Accidental Secret Daddy

A Second Chance Romance

Callie Stevens

Chapter 1

Axel

Returning to my hometown after all those weeks away on tour feels surreal. Everything looks the same, but somehow, it feels different. It might be because I've been in all these big cities performing, but I think mostly is because there is one major difference. Harley isn't here.

Harley Telman has been the love of my life since I was sixteen years old and she moved almost next door to me. From the moment I met her, I couldn't see anyone else. Hell, I *still* can't, no matter how many groupies throw themselves at me.

The tribal tattoo on my arm is a constant reminder of all I had and lost. The dates camouflaged into it mark the happiest days of my life. The day she said yes to being my girl and the day I made her mine forever. Or so I thought. Regardless, Harley will always be a part of me. Like she's imprinted in my very soul.

I shake my head, trying to rid myself of thoughts of her. The pain is too raw still. It has been five months since I saw her last and it still hurts as much as if it had been yesterday.

But I can't dwell on that now because I have an important meeting with a real estate agent.

While I was on tour, things weren't as bad because I had multiple distractions, including endless amounts of booze, the shows, my friends, and the never-ending supply of bed partners. But coming home to the memories of her is crushing me. I can't stay in that house. Our house.

So, I need a new place to stay. Thank God for Theresa, my realtor friend. She told me of this little duplex that should be perfect for me, or so she says. Since I started taking care of social media for the band and recording covers and unplugged versions of our songs, I realized I need a space that will allow me to have a room just for my equipment. The band is doing well, so now is the perfect time to take the risk and buy a new place.

If I weren't doing the social media stuff, a bedroom and a bathroom with a little kitchen would be more than enough, because there is no way I'll ever get to share my life with anyone ever again. In the span of eleven years, I found and lost my soulmate. There is no way I'll ever want anyone other than her.

I don't much look forward to living right next door to someone, but maybe having someone around will help me. After these months of always having the guys and Gemma around, I think I might be lonely living by myself, but it's not like I have much of a choice.

The realtor assures me that the other occupant is a lovely woman, and she hinted that she's around my age. Maybe we can become friends and it'll be fun. At least, that's the hope.

I'm starving by the time I make it to the little duplex that I'm touring on the request of my realtor, and I see her there, smiling and waving, as I pull up on my motorcycle, parking with plenty of room for the U-Haul trailer behind it. I take my helmet off slowly, appreciating the back view of the woman standing in the yard next to Theresa.

Holy shit. She looks good from the back and she's got all this blonde hair in curls down her back, which I have to admit, does something for me. Reminds me of Harley's mane of hair and how much I loved seeing it sprawled on my pillow.

As I approach Theresa, I try to shake myself off thoughts of Harley. My eyes stay on the woman and I realize that she's very pregnant, probably ready to pop. Not sure how friendly we can become if she'll soon have all her time consumed by a mini-human being, but I love people and there is no harm in saying hi, I guess.

At my approach, she turns and smiles at me, as I stop right in front of Theresa and her, holding my helmet in one hand.

When our eyes connect, my helmet drops to the ground.

It has been five long months since the last time I heard her voice. Longer since I looked at her face. And now, here she is, right in front of me, blinking at me with those big blue eyes of hers, and she's *pregnant*.

What the *fuck*?

Chapter 2

Harley

This cannot be happening to me. Axel Jermaine cannot be standing in my yard. And he's staring at my stomach like I have an alien inside me instead of a baby.

"Harley, this is -" Theresa starts, and I hold up my hand to stop her.

"We've met," I say dryly, and Axel barks out a laugh.

"You could say that," he responds, and there's a bite in his voice. He's mad.

I can't really blame him. After all, I have been radio silent for months. I can feel the blood leaving my face, waiting for him to put it together.

"Where is he?" he asks in a clipped tone, although his face doesn't show his distress. Axel's really good at hiding his emotions when the situation calls for it.

I pause, confused, until I finally realize that he thinks I've got some boyfriend or new husband around that got me in this situation, which is both sad and a relief. Sad because he thinks I'd do that. A relief because as long as he thinks that, I don't have to worry about him putting the dates together from the last time we were intimate.

I shrug. "Around."

Theresa stares at me but she doesn't say anything. Bless her.

Theresa Santos and I became close since I moved into the duplex, mostly because I was on my own and terrified, trying to keep my pregnancy a secret from all the people close to me. She knows it's just me and the baby, but she doesn't know my past or who Axel is to me.

All my friends know my history with Axel, and they'd know immediately what was going on, so I isolated myself from them. From everyone, really, preferring to be alone than risking my secret. I'm the only one who can be trusted, because there's no way in hell I ever want my ex-husband to find out he knocked me up.

As much as it pains me and my heart breaks at the thought, Axel and I are done. I had my reasons and those haven't changed. There is no way a baby is going to change things or make them any better.

There's a muscle twitching in Axel's jaw as he keeps staring at me, and something like hurt flashes across his face when he meets my eyes. It's so quick anyone but me would have missed it. I look away, my heart sinking. I'm still too attuned to his moods, as mercurial as they are. And the thought of hurting him hurts me tenfold.

Fuck. I thought I was almost over him. The way my heart is aching tells me I'm wrong.

"Um, is there something I'm missing, here?" Theresa asks.

"Nope," Axel responds. "I'll take it."

My eyes shoot to his, but he won't look at me now.

5

"What do you mean, you'll take it?" I ask, dread filling me. He can't stay here. Axel shrugs.

"It's a nice place. I like the lawn." He hasn't even seen the inside of the duplex.

Anxiety and anger rise inside me. I know he's just doing this to get a rise out of me, that he wants to stay here to try and figure out who got me pregnant. But that can't happen. There is a reason I had to stay away from him. And now I have my baby to think about too. My child needs to be the most important thing in my life now, and I can't focus on her if I have to see him every day.

"Fine, I'll move out," I shoot back, and Theresa gives me a pained look.

"Harley, I'm all booked up for the summer. There isn't a single two-bedroom available anywhere in town," she says slowly.

Fuck. I need a two bedroom for the nursery. As I contemplate what the hell I'm going to do, Axel shakes Theresa's hand and takes the key.

The next thing I know, Theresa is leaving and he's moving boxes out of the U-Haul into the left side of the duplex as I'm standing there, shell-shocked. I watch his biceps bulge as he picks up a large suitcase, and my mind tries to run away from me, taking me back to a different time. A time when we couldn't stand being apart for a second.

I look away. I have to. There is no way I will allow my hormones to get the best of me. Axel Jermaine shattered my heart. Yeah, he's hot, but that's not enough to make up for how he is.

It's not even like Axel is a bad guy. He's a good guy, but just not the right guy for me. I can't handle all the partying and the girls hanging off his arm. It's not that I don't trust him, though Axel has always been a big flirt. It's that I don't trust them. The fans. The women constantly throwing themselves at him. I hate that I am that insecure, but my past growing up taught me that men can't always be trusted, no matter how much you love them or how much they claim to love you.

At first, we were together all the time. From the time I moved a bit down the street from him, he had been enchanted by me. Me? Not so much. His flirty ways always had me doubting if I was enough. From the moment we met, and for four years, we were glued at the hip. Right after he joined the band, he proposed to me, and that was one of the happiest days of my life. Becoming his wife was a dream come true, but it soon became a nightmare.

"When do I get to meet the lucky guy?" Axel asks, jolting me out of my head.

"What?" I ask, confused, and Axel scoffs.

"The daddy. He must be proud," he drawls, and I give him a hard look.

"You won't. He doesn't come around here," I tell him, and Axel stares at me for a long moment.

He takes in a deep breath, and I swear I can tell he's inwardly counting to ten. Axel's always had a temper, and honestly, I'm surprised that he's taking it this well. In fact, it makes my heart sink. If he's barely even jealous, does he even care anymore? Maybe he met someone else on that big tour Jack and the Spades did. And why do I even care, anyway? Why does it crush me to even consider that?

"Good," he grumbles, and I take in a breath of my own.

"What about you? I don't want girls coming in and out of here," I shoot back, and Axel grins.

"Not that you can dictate who I can or can't have in my

house, since I'm paying for rent same as you, but don't worry, sweetheart. They rarely stay the night."

He's right, of course, but that doesn't stop anger from boiling up in me, something bitter at the back of my throat. I huff out a breath and head inside, tears springing to the backs of my eyes. I've always been an angry crier, and I hate that about myself. It's only gotten worse with all the hormones, and I certainly don't want Axel to think I'm upset instead of just mad.

Before I can escape inside, he asks, "How far along are you?"

"Going on seven months," I lie. I'm eight months. It's been precisely eight months, two days, and seventeen hours since this baby was made. Eight months, two days, seventeen hours since I was with a man, but who is counting. Thing is, he can't know that. Ever.

Axel grunts, looking away from me. "You didn't waste any time."

"Why should I? I doubt you did," I retort, and I can feel Axel's sharp blue eyes driving a hole on my back. But I can't face him.

"You think you know everything, don't you, Harl?" he says mysteriously, and his heavy footsteps retreat, probably heading toward the U-Haul.

I take the opportunity to sneak into the house, breathing hard and trying not to cry. When we got married, I had dreamed of a loving family with Axel. Being with him forever, our children running and playing and wreaking havoc all around us as we happily watched them grow. Gently setting my hand on my belly, I contemplate the fact that my dream was an illusion. I know now I'll never stop loving Axel, and this little one is the only part I'll ever have of him. I wish he could be part of this, of us, but his priorities lie elsewhere. And I may not be able to change that but there is no way my baby will grow up feeling like she isn't the most important person in the world. I rather she thinks her dad died or went away than feel like she is an afterthought in his life.

Noise from outside draws my curiosity and it only takes a minute before I get go peeking out of my blinds to see him carrying more boxes inside.

He pauses to tug off his shirt. *Damnit.* I can't seem to look away, watching the muscles in his abdomen and chest as he wipes sweat from his brow with his T-shirt. It reminds me of when he was on stage, after a solo, when he'd grin and throw his sweaty T-shirt right at me. Axel is perfect for lead guitar, perfect for the stage, and for most of my life, I thought he was perfect for me.

I want to call my best friend, Charlotte, but I haven't talked to her in months. She'd even sent me a letter at my parents' house, pleading with me to call her, but I'd kept ignoring her calls, kept telling my mother to tell her that I wasn't feeling well when she finally showed up. I can't call her, as badly as I need my best friend.

Instead, I call Theresa, my only friend now.

"Harley Telman, what the hell is going on with you and Axel?" Theresa answers, and I almost want to laugh.

I'm glad that she's my friend and not just my landlord, that's for sure.

"He's my ex-husband," I say, and Theresa gasps dramatically. She must still be in the car, on the way back to the office, because it's only been an hour since Axel showed up.

"He's your *what?* Is he...is he the father?" she asks.

I bite my lip, thinking, but in the end, I decide that it's best to keep this secret to myself, because no one can slip if no one knows.

9

"No, he's not. He's just a pain in my ass," I respond, and Theresa lets out a low whistle.

"I noticed there was some tension between you two, but I never imagined you used to be *married.*"

"You've got to get him out of here," I say firmly, and Theresa pauses on the line.

"Is he a bad guy? Was it an abusive relationship?"

"No, no," I say instantly. Axel would never lay a hand on me, despite his short temper. That was never the problem. I never doubted his love for me. He was the sweetest, most loving man ever. "Nothing like that. It just didn't work out."

"I can't kick someone out of a duplex they paid for just because you have history with him, Harley. You've got to give me something more," Theresa says with a sigh.

I worry my bottom lip between my teeth. "Then you've got to find me something else, Theresa. I can't live like this, not with him right next door..." Tears start to well in my eyes again and I angrily wipe my eyes. Stupid hormones.

"I'll keep an eye out, but it's going to be a while, Harl. Like I said, everything's booked up for the summer."

I heave a deep sigh. "Thank you for looking."

We chat for another few minutes and then I hang up, rubbing my hands across my face. I look over at the half put together crib in the corner and sigh again. I hate DIYs and I've never been particularly handy.

I can't help myself from peering out the window again, and this time, Axel is on his motorcycle and looking right at me. Part of me wants to snap the blinds closed, but I'm not sure if he can see me from this distance.

There's this pull in my stomach as we meet eyes, some kind of line of fate drawing me back to him, but I push it away. Just like before, something flashes across his face, so quickly anyone else might have missed it. I'm not sure if it's anger or hurt or both, and I almost expect him to get off his bike and come stalking up to the front door.

My breath catches in my throat. Do I *want* him to come to the door? Do I want him to take me in his arms, tell me everything is okay? Yes. No. Maybe...

Finally, he breaks eye contact, putting on his helmet. He takes off, tires squealing as he pulls the motorcycle and the U-Haul into the street.

I finally let out the breath I've been holding and my mind clears. I can't want him. We've been there before and there was only hurt for me at the end. Axel Jermaine, living no more than a hundred feet from me and my baby is a recipe for disaster.

How am I going to get out of this?

Chapter 3

Axel

I empty the U-Haul in record time, trying to burn off all the anger and jealousy that's coursing through me. Harley's *pregnant*. The sight of her distended belly keeps flashing through my mind over and over. She's got someone else's baby in her stomach. She let someone else inside her, let someone else spread her legs, fill her up.

My head pounds with rage and my jaw hurts from gritting my teeth. As far as I know, Harley had only had one boyfriend before me, some jerk named Chadwick, and it was just a couple of hookups when they were kids. We started seeing each other when she was fifteen and I was sixteen. I might not have been her first kiss, but I was her first everything else. Except, I'm not the baby's dad, and there's something so *wrong* about thinking of her with someone else.

It's driving me crazy. My blood feels like it's boiling and I've got no outlet for it. I try to start unpacking, but eventually, I just end up slamming cabinets and throwing boxes. Usually, I'd go to the gym, but since I'm moving, I have to find a new gym. With those months on tour, I let the last

12

gym membership lapse. I set up the television and flip it on, but it doesn't help in the slightest. The sound of my heart pounding in my ears over the sound of the television is deafening. I keep picturing it in my mind, someone else's cock entering Harley. It doesn't help that I remember vividly the way she feels and sounds underneath me, the way her mouth pops open in an "o" of pleasure. The thought of her doing that for someone else makes me want to scream.

Instead, I text Samuel: ***Meet me at the Dirty Dozen?***

The Dirty Dozen is the first dive bar that Jack and the Spades had ever played at, and it became a regular spot for all of us. Samuel and I had always been close since we grew up in the same neighborhood. I nearly cheer when he texts me back: ***Sure.*** If I don't get some tequila in my stomach I might just lose my mind.

I change into a fresh black t-shirt and a pair of tight jeans, noting in the mirror that my eyes are a bit bloodshot. Sleep had been hard to come by on the tour, especially since I'd gotten divorced not long before we embarked on it, and it seems like I'm not going to get much of it tonight, either.

I head out to my bike and hop on, and a ray of light from Harley's side of the duplex catches my eye. When I turn, she's looking at me through the blinds, the light from the kitchen shining through. I can't quite make out the expression on her face, only able to see her big blue eyes. My heart aches so much I can barely stand it, and I think about storming over to confront her. I don't even know what I would say, but everything in me wants to go to her.

Finally, I tear my eyes away, swallowing hard, and put on my helmet. I nearly spin out pulling out onto the highway, but I don't care.

When I arrive at the Dozen, Samuel is already there and he's ordered us a pitcher of Blue Moon. Bless him.

"You're an angel among men, Sam," I tell him, clapping him on the shoulder, and he arches a dark eyebrow.

"What's going on?" he asks, and I groan, sitting on the barstool next to him.

"Harley's pregnant," I say flatly, and Samuel's eyes nearly bulge out of his head.

"She's *what*?" Samuel looks almost as shell shocked as I feel.

"Yep. Seven months. She must have grabbed the first guy who looked at her twice." I feel bad the instant I say it. It's not my business what Harley did after we divorced, but it feels like a betrayal nonetheless.

"You signed the papers, Axel," Samuel comments, taking up for Harley. I can't blame him. He knows her just as well as he knows me, and they'd been friends, too. "You knew this was a possibility."

Yes, I did. But did it have to be as my bed side was still warm? We had been together on last time eight months ago. That is the last time I had seen her until today. And a couple of months after that, she stopped answering my calls, replying to my texts. Could that be why? Had she just hooked up with the first guy who looked at her? It's unkind of me to think of Harley picking out the first guy who hit on her after we divorced, but I can't help feeling bitter. In fact, that's how my mouth tastes, bitter, like I've been sucking on lemons, so I pour myself a glass of beer and drink half of it.

"You should take it easy," Samuel says nervously. "You partied pretty hard on the tour."

I look at Samuel and finish the rest of the glass. "I appreciate your concern, bud, but tonight there's no *way* I'm going to take it easy."

Samuel sighs and orders us two shots of Don Julio with lime and salt.

"I could kiss you," I say, grinning at him and throwing an arm around him, and Samuel pretends to gag.

Samuel clinks his shot glass with mine and takes it, grimacing.

As the alcohol starts to warm my stomach, I feel a tiny bit better and start talking to the bartender. She's pretty, a blonde like Harley, although her hair is probably from a bottle instead of natural.

"My name's Axel," I tell her. "I play lead guitar for Jack and the Spades."

The bartender's eyes widen. "No shit? I just heard you guys on the radio! That song, what's it called?"

"Keyed Up," I say dryly, knowing that it must be the one that Locke penned. The song had become our title track, despite it being a B side. Locke's love affair with our lead singer's little sister had really caused him to be a better songwriter.

"That's the one!" The bartender leans over the bar, showing off her cleavage. I look respectfully before looking back at her face, and she grins.

After all, I am a hot-blooded American male, aren't I?

Maybe tonight's the night that I finally break my dry spell. I know the guys think I sleep around. I certainly act the part. I leave with one or more women after every show and we pick up the party right at our destination, usually one of their houses. But when push comes to shove, I just haven't been able to take that last step. I know I signed the papers. I know I'm divorced. That's clear in my mind, but my heart and my cock haven't gotten the memo. So, I haven't been able to touch anyone, or let anyone touch me. I haven't been with anyone since Harley, and it's beginning to bug me. Especially now that I know she certainly hasn't been celibate.

"I'm Sophie," she purrs, and Samuel rolls his eyes.

"I'm in the band, too," he grumbles, and she favors him with a big smile.

"Nice to meet you, Sophie. You're a wonderful bartender," I flirt, although since she's only served us beer and shots, I don't know what kind of bartender she is.

"I only do this on the side. I'm a singer," she tells me, and slides another two shots to us. She winks. "On the house for my favorite band."

Samuel stares at the shot like it might bite him, but I take mine, biting down on the lime afterward. The tequila and beer are starting to do their job, making my head fuzzy and my heartache less painful.

"A singer? Lucky me, I could use a backup singer for one of the video posts I'm doing for the band," I tell her. This is turning into more of a work conversation than a romantic one, but I don't mind. Anything that keeps my mind off Harley and that bun in her oven that I didn't put there.

"Really? I'd love to show you some of my stuff," she says excitedly, ignoring the two guys who just walked up to the end of the bar. "Maybe we could work together."

"I should be so lucky," I drawl, and she grins at me again. She really is pretty, although her eyes are brown instead of blue, like Harley's.

Somewhere around the fourth shot, everything goes hazy and the room starts spinning.

Samuel is in the bathroom, probably puking up his guts. He doesn't have half the tolerance I do. I usually wouldn't be this drunk, but I haven't eaten today.

"I get off work in thirty minutes. Why don't I take you home, handsome?"

I'm holding myself up by bracing my hands on the bar, so I figure that's a great idea.

"You don't mind me crashing at your place?" I try to be careful not to slur my words, but it's a losing battle.

"You're gorgeous," Sophie gushes. "Plus, I'm hoping that you'll give me a job."

"You're hired," I tell her, and the next thing I know she's pushing me into her car. I'm not quite sure how we got there, but I'm not complaining.

My head lolls against the seat and finally the pounding in my ears has calmed down. I feel a little nauseous due to not eating, but the motion of the car doesn't make me worse.

I reach out to touch her blonde hair, curling it around the ends of my fingers.

Harley. I remember her waking up in bed next to me, sitting straight up when the alarm sounds instead of hitting the snooze button like I do every morning.

"Good morning, sunshine!" She'd chirp, bouncing on the bed to wake me, and I'd groan and slip my arms around her waist, pulling her close.

Tears spring to the backs of my eyes and I rub my hands across my face.

"Are you okay?" Sophie asks, and I bark out a laugh.

"No," I admit, and she looks at me, concerned.

"Are you going to ralph in my car?"

I shake my head and the world spins on its axis. "I don't think so."

"Okay, then." She sings along to the radio as she takes me back to her apartment, and I fade in and out of consciousness, having dreams about Harley's sleepy blue eyes first thing in the morning.

17

By the time we get to her place, she has to help me inside, groaning as she puts me on the couch.

"It's too bad that you're too drunk to hook up," she whines, and I look up at her.

"Who said that?" I ask stubbornly, trying to sit up straight.

"Something about the way you called me Harley twice," she drawls, and I chuckle low in my throat.

"Okay, Sophie. Work it is, I guess. Sing something for me."

She stares at me, wide eyed. "Right now?"

I nod, managing to sit up straighter. The movement clears my head a little.

She sings a few bars of "Keyed Up," and she really does have a good voice. She's an alto, which will mix well with my baritone.

I spend the rest of the night talking with her about music and we even do some recording. At least I'm not still dreaming about Harley.

Chapter 4

Harley

Despite not getting much sleep because I couldn't stop thinking about the fact that my ex-husband moved into my duplex yesterday, I get up early. I don't sleep much anyway, now that the baby has gotten so big. I'm still working because I need money for the baby since I sure as hell won't ask Axel for alimony. I just wanted to be rid of him, even though he is making that difficult.

My stomach growls as I drive past a new diner that's opened up in the last few weeks, and I swing into the parking lot. The baby demands food, I get it. That's how things work around here. I don't mind, not really. This baby is my reason to live now. She is why I wake up every morning and am able to get out of bed, why I'm able to work, to move on.

I don't know for sure if the baby is a girl—he or she has been shy and hasn't been playing exhibitionist during ultrasounds, so it's a guessing game at this point, but I just have a feeling. I haven't even thought about names. Hell, I haven't even gotten her crib together, yet. I've been feeling so alone and overwhelmed, taking each day as it comes and dealing with the now, so I don't have to face the fact that I'm all this baby will ever have.

The only problem with that is that I haven't done nearly enough to get ready for this baby. I have about one month to go, give or take, and I don't even have her crib ready. This baby is my priority, my world, but I've just been so tired, so alone.

The inside of the diner smells amazing, like smoked prime rib, and that's the special for the day, according to the sign. My mouth waters instantly until the sound of an awfully familiar low chuckle breaks through my hunger.

I turn to the sight of a blonde leaning over a booth, smiling widely at my ex-husband.

My mouth turns bitter, and I can taste acid at the back of my throat. *I'm not jealous*, I tell myself. *I'm just pregnant and hungry.* I clear my throat and Axel turns toward me.

"Oh, hey, Harls," he drawls, as if he's not sitting across from some bimbo.

Hiding the shattering of my heart, I huff out a breath and ignore him, ordering a prime rib sandwich with tater tots at the counter. Axel comes up behind me and the hair on the back of my neck stands up as he murmurs in my ear.

"Fancy meeting you here."

"Let me guess, breakfast with the new squeeze?" My voice sounds clipped and angry even to my own ears, but I can't bring myself to care. I know he's been out all night because I didn't see his motorcycle in the driveway. He smells faintly of tequila, which doesn't surprise me in the least.

"Jealous, sweetheart?" he asks, the pet name sounding familiar on his lips.

"No. Just don't bring her to the house at three in the morning and we'll be fine," I spit out.

Axel chuckles. "You *are* jealous. A bit hypocritical, don't you think?"

I turn to look at him and he's looking down at my swollen belly. I swallow hard.

"I told you; I'm not jealous. I just need my rest since the baby is coming soon," I argue, and Axel takes a step back.

"I guess you do, being a single mom and all that," Axel says, a bitter tone to his low voice.

"That's none of your business."

How long did it take to put a prime rib sandwich together? I jiggle my leg anxiously. I don't know how I'm going to live right next to him when I can't stand being in the same room with him for five minutes. I really mean it when I say I don't want him bringing girls over, and although I can tell him and myself it's because I need my rest, I know that's not true. I need my sanity, and it will drive me absolutely bonkers to hear him making someone else moan.

"Nothing seems to be my business anymore," Axel comments.

"That's how divorce works, Axel. We split up and nothing I do should matter to you anymore," I say firmly, not looking at him. I don't want to see it flash across his face, that look of shock and hurt. It makes my heart ache, and I don't want to think about how I'm not over him nearly as much as I think I am.

"You're probably right. Which means things go both ways, Harley. So, if your life is none of my business, what I do is none of yours, including who I invite or don't invite over to my house. If that's how you want it, then that's how it is," Axel says flatly.

"That's how it is," I respond, and nearly snatch the to-go bag out of the server's hand, throwing cash at her and telling her to keep the change. I do my best not to look at the blonde in the booth that Axel is with, rushing out of the diner and making it to the car before tears start to spill from my eyes. Because he is right. I can't make any demands or stop him from taking girls home, but damnit, it will kill me if he does.

As tears start streaming down my face, I wipe them away angrily. *Stupid hormones.*

I don't lie to myself often, but when I do, it's a doozy. I keep trying to tell myself that I'm over Axel Jermaine, that I don't lie awake at night and wonder whose arms he's in, that it's just the hormones that are making me so emotional. I know the truth, though.

I still love him, always have, and I don't know what the hell I'm going to do about it because I can't go back. Because nothing has really changed from when I left, and I can't stand the fact that he doesn't care anymore.

I take in a deep breath and back the car out of the parking lot, heading to my job that it's closer and closer to be put on hold. It's getting harder and harder to move around and sitting all day is not good for me or the baby, so soon I'll have to ask for my leave. I tell myself it's just one more week, because I really do need the money, but I know I'll work until this baby pops if that's what it takes to keep both my sanity and support her better.

I would ask my parents for help if I were desperate, but I don't want to burden them. They are retired and living the life, though dad still consults sometimes, which keeps him busy and happy. Mom says she enjoys the peace and quiet and her 'me' time while he is gone.

I arrive at work and my coworker, Roland, gives me a big smile. I smile back weakly.

"How was your weekend?" he asks. Roland has always

been nice to me, and I want to do my best not to lash out at him, but I can't help feeling grumpy after what just happened.

"I don't want to talk about it," I mumble, and he arches a dark eyebrow, but doesn't say anything, bless him.

"I bought you some decaf," he says softly, pushing it toward me, and I take it gratefully.

"Thanks, Roland." I take a sip and I miss the jolt of caffeine, but it's not good for the baby. Roland is sweet enough to know that.

I know he has a thing for me, but I can't imagine dating anyone while I'm this pregnant with another man's baby. If I'm truthful to myself, the thought of being with anyone other than Axel is unconceivable. Besides, my baby is my life now, so there will be no man in my life anytime soon, unless in the colleague or friend capacity, and I'm just fine with that.

Roland looks at me like he wants to ask more questions, but he doesn't, and I'm grateful for it. I don't feel like talking, even to someone as nice as him. He's cute, in his own way that's totally different than Axel, but I just can't bring myself to be attracted to anyone else.

Axel has a hold on me, and I can't deny that, even to myself. I remember seeing him shirtless, tattoos on display and muscles bulging, and I take in a deep breath through my nostrils, trying to rid myself of the memory.

It's hard because it's not like Axel was awful to me. He was just more focused on his career than on us. And while I'd had no problem with it when life allowed me to accompany him, things had changed and he wouldn't compromise. Him staying out all night, all the social media Gemma posted of him flirting with fans onstage while I had to stay home had driven a wedge between us. Seeing him this morning only proved to me that he's the same man he always was–staying out all night and having breakfast with some girl he met the night before.

Theresa calls me around noon.

"Please tell me you found me a place to live," I answer excitedly.

"Nothing like that, Harley, sorry. I was just calling to check on you," Theresa answers, and I heave a deep sigh.

"It's not that I'm not grateful you're checking up on me, but I was *really* hoping that I could get out of here soon."

"No such luck, babes. I know it must be hard for you, living right next door to him. I just wanted to make sure you were okay."

I groan. "You have no idea. He didn't come home last night."

"Isn't that a good thing? At least he wasn't there. Wasn't that what you wanted?"

"I guess, but this morning I saw him at a diner with some woman."

Theresa whistles in sympathy. "That must be hard. Things seemed really tense between you two."

"For months after the divorce, he wanted us to get back together, but I kept pushing him back. And I haven't even answered his calls or texts in months. Until I saw him again, I thought I was over him," I say glumly. "I guess I was kidding myself. And looking at him this morning, looked like he had finally moved on."

Theresa pauses on the line, and I can hear her breathing. "So... Why don't you try talking to him? Maybe even try to work things out?"

"No, our time has passed," I say resolutely. "We've been doing this dance since I was sixteen, and though life changes, he never did. I can't put my baby through that."

Theresa sighs. "I guess that makes sense. Do you want to come over, have a girl's night? Some popcorn and a rom com?'

"No romance. A horror movie. Something bloody," I insist, and Theresa chortles.

"Fair enough. I'll pick you up from work."

"You're an angel, Theresa," I say gratefully. "I gotta go, lunch break is over."

"See you at five!" Theresa chirps.

I let out a relived breath. My chest felt tight, and now everything is loosening up a little.

Maybe this is just what I need to get my mind off Axel Jermaine.

Chapter 5

Axel

I call Samuel first, knowing that I won't be able to be alone tonight. I'll end up drinking too much beer by myself and go to Harley and beg her to take me back. I have my dignity, after all.

"What about a garage jam session?" I ask him, and Samuel groans.

"I don't know, Locke has been so busy with Gemma and preparing for the baby, and Jackson—"

"I'll convince them," I say firmly, and I plan to. They're my brothers, more than just my band members, after all, and I need them.

Samuel grumbles on the line but I know that he's going to give in, and I grin.

"Fine, if you get everyone there, I'll be there," he says, and I whoop.

"Jack and the Spades reunion is on!"

"You act like we broke up, or something." Samuel laughs. "We are still doing gigs here and there. Gemma is handling all the contacts to see when and where we'll start."

After I get off the line with Samuel, I go to the local

liquor store and pick up a case of beer. I swear that I'm not following Harley, but I see her in the aisle, holding a bottle of sparkling cider and frowning at the label.

I tell myself not to go over to her, but I can't help riling her up. She always hated it when we rehearsed in the garage.

"Just a heads up, I invited the guys over tonight," I tell her, and she looks up at me with an exasperated expression.

"Are you following me?" she asks, and I snort.

"Nah, I'm past that point in my life," I tell her, because not too long ago, there was definitely a time that I was following her around, asking her to talk to me, after we split. "But this is a small town, sweetheart, and we're neighbors. You should get used to seeing me."

"At least I don't have to tonight," she shoots back, and I raise an eyebrow.

"What, you got a hot date?" I ask, not thinking that she really does.

"Wouldn't you like to know?" She smirks up at me, and my blood starts to heat up.

"Really? Dating, in your condition?" I ask her incredulously, and she just shrugs.

I take in a deep breath through my nostrils to calm myself and I shrug back.

"Like you said, it's none of my business," I mumble, and head toward the checkout counter.

My good mood dissipates, just like that. Harley going on a date? I know that I'll be checking through the blinds every half hour until she gets back. And what if she doesn't get back? What if she stays the night?

"Fuck," I curse as I put the beer into my backpack and put it on, getting onto my motorcycle. I hate this, being apart from her, not knowing who she's with or what she's

27

doing. I'd never been particularly jealous while we were together, but this feels so different, so final. She's already pregnant with someone else's kid, so why wouldn't she go on dates?

I'm two beers deep by the time Jackson and Locke roll up, with Samuel only fifteen minutes behind them.

"Spades!" I greet them, pulling Locke into a hug.

The bigger man wrinkles his nose. "You smell like tequila and depression."

"That's the smell of divorce," Jackson comments, and I glare at him.

"Thanks a lot," I mumble, cracking open another beer and handing it to him. Jackson takes one and Locke declines with a groan.

"Gemma's pregnant so I'm not drinking in solidarity."

"Whipped," I mutter, and Jackson chokes on his beer, laughing.

Samuel walks toward us, his bass guitar slung across his back, and everyone yells about his close-cropped hair.

"You joining the army?" Jackson asks, his own blond hair tied back in a ponytail.

"Shut up, I hate you guys," Samuel grumbles, but there's no bite in it.

I feel my mood starting to lift again, and it's not just the beer. Being around the band members has always been where I feel most at home, and it's no different now. Half of the jam session would be drinking and bullshitting, like usual, and half would be real work, and I'm excited about it.

That is, until Samuel opens his big mouth.

"Where's Harley?"

Jackson and Locke stare at me and Locke clears his throat before speaking.

"Are you and Harley back together?"

"No," I say bitterly. "She just happens to be living in the other duplex."

"What the *fuck*?" Jackson curses, and I nod.

"Yeah, I got here, and she was standing in the yard." I pause, sipping my beer. "And she's pregnant."

Locke is staring at me curiously. "Axel, when's the last time you and Harley were together?"

I wave my hand. "It's been a little over eight months. She's only seven months, so the timing doesn't add up."

Locke seems suspicious, but I'm not. Harley wouldn't lie to me about something like that, no matter what my friends might think.

"This isn't a good place for you, Axel," Jackson says, his brows furrowed together. I know that they're worried about me after I partied so hard on tour.

I sigh. "It's okay. I'm over it. We've been divorced for a while now. Eight months and almost a week, I'd say, since we signed the papers... But who is counting, right?"

None of the band members look like they believe me even slightly, and I don't exactly believe myself.

"C'mon, let's get everything set up," I insist, no longer wanting to bullshit if it's going to be about Harley.

We set up the amps and other equipment and everything's a little off-key at first, but we get the hang of it. I'm blasting out a solo when I see a Volkswagen Beetle like Harley's drives drive by, and I miss my cue entirely as it gets to the end of the road. I should have known she's not the only one driving a bug in this part of town.

I shake my head. "Sorry, let's go again. From the top."

We practice until my calloused fingers feel like they're going to fall off, and finally Locke throws down his drumsticks.

"I gotta get back home, I promised Gemma a foot

29

massage. She is getting bigger and her back and feet hurt all the time, so I try and make her feel better any way I can."

"Locke Kincaid, a family man. I never thought I'd see the day," I tease, and Jackson nudges me.

"Hey, he better be a family man and take care of my little sister," Jackson complains, and Samuel nods.

"Gemma's like a little sister to all of us, so you better keep your shit together," Samuel warns.

Locke groans. "Yeah, I got a band of big brothers to keep me in line, but Gemma does the job just fine."

"That's my girl," I grin, and Locke glares at me. My harmless flirting with Gemma on tour hadn't impressed him much, it turns out.

Locke leaves first, and then Jackson, begging off so that he can go meet some girl. He hasn't told us anything about her, but we suspect he has been hooking with the same girl throughout the whole tour, and they are still going. Lucky bastard. We're down to the last four beers in the case and I crack another one open.

Samuel grimaces. "It has to be warm by now."

I shrug. "Still does the job."

"You keep acting like Harley living next door is no big deal, but I know it is," Samuel starts, and I roll my eyes.

"Don't act like a girl," I tell him, but he's right. It's a *very* big deal, and since it's nearing ten at night, I keep waiting for her car to pull up the street.

Samuel gives me a look and I finally sigh.

"I saw her today and she implied she was going on a date. I can't stand to even think about it," I admit.

Samuel snorts. "She's not going on a date. She's just trying to rile you up. You know how she gets. She used to shit like this in high school. Remember, for a whole week, she had you convinced that she and I were a thing."

I growl. "I almost hit you."

Samuel grins. "I remember, you threw me up against the locker before she stopped you. Don't worry about it, it's all an act."

I feel better for a moment, but then I remember her swollen belly and deflate, gulping down my beer as if there might be an answer at the bottom.

"I don't know, Sam. It's different, now. She's pregnant, for God's sake."

Samuel claps me on the shoulder. "I'm sorry, man. Look, I gotta get out of here, I have some shit to do in the morning. Promise me you won't drink the rest of those beers and wait up for Harley."

"I think you know I can't promise that, Sammy," I say mock-cheerfully, and Samuel rolls his eyes as he packs up his bass guitar. Jackson took the microphone and Locke took his drum set, so the garage seems oddly empty other than a few boxes that Harley had there.

I look over at them, wondering what's in them. After Samuel leaves and I have another beer, I figure she'll be none the wiser. I sit down on the ground and go through the first box, and the photo album I find makes my breath catch in my throat.

It's our wedding album. I flip through the pictures of Harley looking beautiful in her white dress, my heart aching. There are pictures of Jack and the Spades, too, where we'd performed as a wedding act. I'd written a song just for Harley. There's dust on the outside of the photo album and I hate seeing it. All these memories just thrown away in the garage. It hurts deep in my bones somewhere, that she put them out here, that she just doesn't care.

When her Volkswagen Beetle pulls into the driveway at one in the morning, I've switched to tequila, which might not have been a great idea, and I still have the album in my lap.

"So, now you're going through my stuff?" she says with a sigh. She's wearing makeup, and she's still wearing her work clothes, at least.

"It's *our* stuff," I snarl, unable to hold back the anger that's been boiling in me all night. "You just threw it out here in a box like it was garbage."

"It's over, Axel. It's done. How many times do I have to tell you that?" She's standing by the door.

I stand up, less steadily than I would have liked to, striding toward her. She shrinks against the door, but I know she's not afraid of me.

"I guess you'll have to tell me again. Look me in the eye, Harley. Tell me again that it's over."

Harley's face is screwed up with frustration and she turns those blue eyes up to mine. She opens her mouth, and I take the opportunity to lean down and kiss her.

I wait for her to punch me, to push me away, but instead, she moans into my mouth, sliding her tongue between my lips.

Chapter 6

Harley

I know I shouldn't do this. I know that I should push him away, that I should yell in his face, look him right in the eye and tell him that it's really over. I can't get my hands and arms to move. I can't bring myself to open my mouth and tell him no. I've always had a hard time resisting Axel, and it seems the divorce and our time apart didn't change things.

"You still taste like cinnamon," Axel groans, moving his mouth to my neck and kissing me there.

I still chew Big Red gum every day.

"You taste like tequila," I say, and that's familiar too. It's familiar enough that it makes me think that I *should* push him away, but his hands are roving over my arms, down to my hips, and it feels so good to be touched.

"I can't stop drinking since you left me. You're driving me fucking crazy," Axel growls, biting down on my neck and I let out an involuntary moan.

"I am?" I ask, because I have been wondering about it, especially since I've seen him with someone else just this morning.

Axel pulls away to look at me, his blue eyes hazy from booze.

"You *know* you do, Harls. I've been a mess since you left, and now..." He looks down at my belly, and I bite my lip.

"You wouldn't even want me now," I whisper, and Axel scoffs.

"I'll always want you, Harley. You could never do anything to make me *not* want you," he says fiercely, and he kisses me again.

My arms go around his neck as if they have a mind of their own, and I can't help opening my mouth, letting his tongue slide in next to mine. The bitter taste of tequila mixes well with the cinnamon, somehow, making me want more. I press my body against his. Axel's nearly pins me against the wall, his hands all over me. He cups my breasts and I gasp into his mouth.

"Let me in," Axel pleads. "Let me in, just tonight."

I know that I need to stop. I know that I need to say no.

"Just tonight," I say firmly, and Axel grins. He knows he's got me, there's no way I'm going to let him into my duplex and turn him down.

He steps back long enough for me to unlock the door, and when I get inside, his hands are all over my ass and thighs as I put my purse down and slip off my shoes.

"I missed you so much, sweetheart," he mumbles in my ear, his words only a little slurred around the edges. I don't want to think about how much he's had to drink, or how much his tolerance must have gone up since we split up.

I saw the case of beer in the garage and the bottle of tequila he was holding when I first came in.

I don't respond, throwing my keys on the counter, but then Axel is lifting me up, seemingly having no problem even though I'm much heavier than I was the last time we hooked up. He places me gently on the kitchen counter, pulling at my thigh-highs to get them off me and leaning down to suck marks onto my skin.

I gasp out his name, my legs spreading automatically. God, it has been so long since he's touched me that my skin is singing under his hands and mouth. I feel like I'm going to explode. Pregnancy hormones haven't taken away my sex drive the way I thought it would. On the contrary. I've been feeling cranky as a result of sexual frustration.

Axel's mouth feels like fire as he leaves a series of kisses on my inner thighs, and with no warning, he buries his face in my sex. I brace my hands on the counter behind me, moaning, as his nose bumps my clit.

He laps at my entrance, those intense blue eyes of his looking up at me from between my thighs. I have to lean up to see him over the swell of my stomach, but Axel doesn't seem to mind.

He moves his mouth up to suction around my clit and I gasp out his name. Axel hums happily against me, moving his right hand from my thigh to slide his index and middle finger inside me.

I nearly shout in pleasure before I clap my hand over my mouth. Axel makes a sound of displeasure in the back of his throat and stands up, moving my hand from my mouth.

"I want to hear you, sweetheart. Want to hear it's me that's making you feel so good." His voice is low and raspy from the late hour and the alcohol, and it makes heat pool in my stomach. I'm already slick enough to be embarrassed, but when Axel angles his fingers up, kissing the base of my throat, I let out a long moan.

I guess I don't have neighbors to worry about since my neighbor is the one making me make all these wanton noises. My head feels fuzzy, as if I've had a few glasses of wine at dinner although I haven't had a drop. I'm drunk on Axel, on the way he makes me feel, and I know this is dangerous.

I could still stop this. I could still push him away and tell him that I changed my mind, tell him that we can't do this.

"Axel," I gasp, and his eyes snap to mine.

"Say it again," he commands, and his voice sends a jolt of pleasure through me as he pushes his fingers deeper.

"Axel," I repeat, louder, and I mean to tell him to back off, to tell him that we should stop, but he leans forward and bites my neck. My head goes fuzzy all over again.

"I could make you come right here on this counter," Axel says, and I almost feel dizzy with lust, letting out a low whimper.

"Please," I plead. "Please, your fingers feel so good."

"My cock will feel better." Axel slowly removes his fingers and I pant, feeling empty, wanting more.

I start to hop off the counter, not wanting him to lift me and grunt with effort, but he scoops me up anyway, as if I'm light as a feather. I've gained nearly thirty pounds during my pregnancy, but Axel acts as if I weigh nothing at all.

He holds me tightly around my ass and thighs, my belly bumping against his. I'm almost embarrassed, but I guess I'm too far gone, because all I can do is wrap my arms around his neck to help him carry me.

He deposits me on the bed gently, crawling toward me, and I spread my legs in anticipation.

"I wanted to taste you all night, but I don't think I can wait, sweetheart," he groans. "It's been so long...."

"Please, please," I plead, and I hate that I've lost all dignity so quickly, but there's just something about the way he touches me, something about the way he makes love to me.

Something about it feels like coming home, although I can't say that to him.

Axel shifts, fumbling a bit with the button of his jeans before pushing them down over his ass, finally freeing himself with a groan. He's not huge, but Axel's always been well-endowed, more girthy than he is long, and it's always felt perfect to me.

We fit together like puzzle pieces, and it's the same when he pushes into me, looping my knees over his considerable biceps. I look at the swirls there, the tribal I know has our dates in it, and close my eyes, not wanting to think anymore.

Axel takes my chin in his hands, pressing down on either side of my jaw to pop my mouth open before leaning down to kiss me, sticking his tongue in my mouth sloppily.

"Look at me. I want you to know who's making love to you, who's making you come," he demands, and my eyes pop open.

"Axel," I say again, as if I'm unable to say anything else, and he smirks.

"That's right, sweetheart," he croons, and starts to move his hips. My belly is in the way, and I huff out a frustrated breath when I can't get him deep enough.

Once upon a time, I would have locked my ankles around his waist, pulled him in deeper, but I can't do that in my condition.

As if he's reading my mind, Axel pulls out of me, holding one of my ankles in his hand to turn me over onto my side and sliding up behind me, his mouth on my neck, his breath hot on my flesh.

He lifts my leg up and slides back into me and I moan so

loudly I'm glad we don't have close neighbors. It's more intimate like this, him buried inside me with his body pressed up against mine. I remember us doing this position before, on sleepy mornings before I had to go into work.

"I missed you so fucking much," Axel moans into my ear, voice hoarse, and I turn my head to kiss him, my heart aching.

The thing is, for all the resentment I feel, I miss him too, so much that I can't even express it. It doesn't matter, now, anyway. This is a one-time thing, just a small reprieve that I can allow myself, and then it will be over.

Axel is sucking marks onto my skin, so much that I'll probably have to wear a turtleneck to work tomorrow, but I can't bring myself to complain.

His breathing is getting shorter and I know he's close, but so am I so I roll my hips back against him, crying out when I finally reach my peak, his name coming from my lips over and over like a chant.

"Fuck, you're so hot and tight around me, sweetheart. Sucking me in," Axel pants, and he bites down on my shoulder when he spills inside me in ropes.

I squeeze my eyes shut, breathing hard, and then Axel starts to kiss the marks he'd left on my skin, soft and sweet. After I catch my breath, I turn to tell him that he should go, to push him away, but his eyes are closed, his eyelashes fanning across his cheekbones.

I could tell him to go, shake him awake, kick him out of my bed. I *should*.

But I like the way he feels, softening inside me, his arms tight around my waist, just above the swell of my belly.

This is the way it should be, something in the back of my head says, but instead of listening, I close my eyes and manage to drift off to sleep.

Chapter 7

Axel

W hen I open my eyes, I wonder if last night was a dream. Harley isn't in my arms the way she had been when I fell asleep. The bed feels empty and unfamiliar, but that's not unusual since I've just set up my bed in a new place. I look around, frowning, and realize that I'm not in my duplex, even though Harley's place looks so similar it's no wonder I'm confused.

Not to mention the tequila I'd downed, looking at our wedding pictures. It comes back to me in flashes, kissing Harley's frowning mouth, how she'd invited me inside.

"Fuck," I curse, but it's almost in wonder instead of in anger. I wonder if things will be different, now, if I'll smell her cooking bacon in the kitchen, see her in one of my old T-shirts the way it used to be, the curve of her ass tempting me.

When I sit up, my head pounds and I groan softly.

A bottle of painkillers hits me in the chest and I look up to see Harley standing there in a pair of overalls and a tank top, the swell of her belly reminding me that things aren't as different as I'd been imagining.

She's frowning at me, just like she did the night before, but my mouth has made marks like purple blossoms all the way around her neck, and I can't help but grin.

"Your boyfriend gonna be mad about all the marks I left?" I know it's a low blow and the words feel bitter in the back of my throat. My heart seems to be slowly sinking in my chest the more I wake up.

"I don't have a boyfriend," she snaps, rifling through her clothes in the closet, and I tilt my head.

"Date didn't go well?" I hope it hasn't. I hope he was a total asshole, or better yet, a dud, so boring she could barely stand it.

"I'm not talking about this with you," she mutters, sliding on a pair of flats. "Get out. I have to go to work."

I'm not surprised that she's pissed off, but I have to admit that I expected a little more softness after what happened last night. I feel stupid for thinking anything could change so easily. But then again, I didn't make it easy on her going on the attack when I saw her scowl.

"Harley," I start, and she storms toward the door, opening it wide.

"You have to go, Axel. I'm serious." She *looks* serious, her brows furrowed together, her little chin upturned.

"Fine," I finally mumble, standing up a bit unsteadily and walking toward the door. I'd been barefoot when she'd returned last night, but I was still in all my clothes. I remember vaguely being unable to even think when I'd kissed her, just reacting.

I hope that maybe she'll follow me into the garage, get into her car so that I can see her a bit longer, talk to her. It's pathetic, how I feel about Harley, how I want her around all the time despite the baby in her belly that someone else has put there.

But I've always been that way about her, haven't I? I hate to think it, but nothing's changed since we were sixteen years old.

"We're not going to talk about this?" I ask her as I step out into the garage, and she shakes her head and slams the door in my face.

"God*damnit!*" I yell, storming back into my duplex where boxes are still strewn around the room. I haven't even begun to unpack, and I've already fucked everything up. I should have never kissed her, but she let me do it. She kissed me back. She put her arms around my neck just like she had a thousand times before...

I look at the counter where I have a couple of bottles of tequila and my stomach rumbles. I don't even remember if I ate the day before, and I feel lightheaded from the hangover already. There's nothing in the fridge, either, since I haven't gone grocery shopping.

I walk out to the garage, half of me hoping that Harley will still be there, but she's already gone, her Beetle missing. I get on my bike and put on my helmet, driving too fast to the diner around the corner. I feel antsy, reckless, like I should be doing something more to get her back. I don't know how to make her understand that we're meant to be together.

I'm angry, of course, about the baby and that she let someone else inside her, but we were split up so I can't really complain, as much as I hate it. I hope whoever knocked her up sees those marks all over her throat. I hope he sees it and it's a punch in the gut, just like it is for me every time I see her swollen belly.

At the diner, there's a blonde standing at the counter and I walk up behind her, just waiting in line. She turns and I recognize her face. Susan? Sarah?

"Sophie," she tells me helpfully, smiling widely. "I figure you were too drunk the other day to remember my name."

She sticks out her hand and I shake it, smiling back.

"Sophie with the velvet voice, how could I forget?" Fuck it, I might as well flirt with someone else since Harley doesn't seem to care.

Sophie giggles and she really is pretty. It's too bad that I can't see anyone but Harley. "I thought you were going to offer me a job, but I forgot to give you my number when we came here the next day."

I consider it for a long moment. I *do* need someone to sing backup vocals, particularly in TikToks for promotion. For a while, Gemma said that she would do it, but Locke shut that down pretty quickly. I guess he's still mad that I flirted with her on tour.

"What are you doing after this?" I ask her, and Sophie grins.

An hour later, Sophie is sitting on a box in the garage with me, with my camera and lights set up for social media. Filming in the garage isn't ideal because of the lighting, but until I get something set up in the den of the duplex, it'll have to do.

I strum my guitar to make sure it's tuned correctly and Sophie sips water, getting ready. I play the opening bars of a popular pop song that I've changed to a rock vibe, and Sophie laughs.

"I love this song!"

She's bubbly and cheery in a way I didn't expect, and I find myself smiling back. She sings the first few bars off key, but then sips more water and tries again. This time, it's near perfect, and I wish that we'd already been recording instead of practicing.

"You ready?" I ask her, and she comes to sit behind me, waiting for me to start the opening bars.

The song goes off with only a couple of stops and starts. Sophie yells every time she misses a cue, which I have to admit is pretty cute. I stop thinking about Harley for a few hours, and that's better than all the tequila in my duplex.

It's around dusk when we finish up, recording two TikToks which I'll post according to Gemma's schedule. I put all her information in my phone, including her TikTok screenname so that I can tag her.

"That was so much fun," Sophie gushes, her hand on my arm, and she doesn't lean in and ask for more, like most of our fans did while I was on tour. I smile back at her, and then my heart sinks when she leans in to me.

I turn my head, letting her lips land on my cheek instead of my mouth, and since I have the worst luck in the world, that's when Harley pulls her Beetle into the driveway.

Luckily, we've already cleaned up all of the equipment, or Harley would have run right into the lights' setup. She gets out of the car, slamming the door, her face all screwed up in anger.

"I asked you not to bring girls here," she says in a low, calm voice, and since I know Harley, I know that's more dangerous than if she was yelling.

I stand up and Sophie remains seated, wide eyed. "It's not three AM, which, if I remember correctly, was the timeline you issued, besides, I'm working. Even if I wasn't, there is the little matter of the fact that we established I pay rent just like you and it really is none of your business just like what you do isn't mine, as you so gracefully reminded me," I say in a clipped voice.

She gasps, her eyes widening slightly. Before storming inside her house she mutters something that sounds like, "Looks like work, all right."

She threw me out this morning, keeps giving me the cold shoulder, attacking me left and right, and now she wants to dictate who I can and can't invite over? I'm pissed, but more than that, I'm hurt. And no, I'm not proud of having been blunt with her, but fuck it. I need to let her know it is not okay to treat me like this. I have feelings. And I can't bring a friend or co-worker home when she just went and slept with the first guy she saw right after I signed those divorce papers. I bet the ink hadn't even dried yet!

I heave a deep sigh and Sophie looks up at me with wide brown eyes.

"I didn't know you had a girlfriend."

"I don't," I mutter, and Sophie gives me a look like she doesn't believe me. I sigh again. "She's my ex-wife."

"Oh, shit." Sophie stands up. "I guess that means it's my cue to go."

I nod. "Sorry."

Sophie tilts her head, smiling. "It's okay. Thank you for the gig."

"I'll Cash App you," I promise, and she heads on her merry way, getting into the little Honda she parked on the street.

I stare after her for a moment, wondering what to do. My feelings from just a while ago come roaring back with a vengeance. Harley kicked me out this morning as if last night meant absolutely nothing to her, but now she's mad that I have a woman over? That I'm *working*?

Anger boils in me and I bang on her door loudly. I have to do it twice before she comes to the door, staring up at me, this time in a turtleneck and A-line skirt. She must have changed before she left for work. That makes me even madder, somehow, that she's ashamed of the marks I left.

"If we're going to live like this, you can't talk to me like that in front of my guests, no matter who they are," I say coldly, and Harley glares up at me, her blue eyes flashing.

"This is *my* house," she says, and I scoff.

"Newsflash! I pay the rent here just like you do, sweetheart. I don't think the contract came with a nag." I know that my words are cruel but I can't bring myself to stop. I'm hurt and pissed, damnit.

"Oh, fuck you," she says under her breath, almost in a whisper, and she tries to slam the door but I stick my foot in it so she can't. She glares at me again. "Get out," she whispers.

"Don't tell me what to do." Harley opens her mouth and I kiss her again, just like I did last night.

At first, she melts into me, her arms creeping up, but then she puts both hands on my chest and pushes me, making me stumble backward. She slams the door before I can say anything else, and I want to scream.

Instead, I punch the drywall next to her door, putting a dent in it with my fist and scraping my knuckles up pretty badly. Blood trails down my arm and I curse.

Harley swings the door back open. "What the hell was-" She sees the blood dripping down my arm and her face pales.

"Get in here," she mutters, tugging my good arm, and I stumble inside.

She bustles around for a moment, going to the bathroom

to get some rubbing alcohol and bandages, muttering something under her breath that I can't quite make out.

"I'm not going to apologize," I tell her firmly, and she rolls her eyes, pressing a bandage wet with alcohol on my scraped knuckles. I hiss.

"Wouldn't dream of asking you to," she tells me, dabbing the alcohol on my wound. "Why did you punch the door, you idiot?"

"I was mad," I say simply. There isn't another explanation for it. I'm mad all the time, anger and pain boiling up in me, and it's because of her.

"Next time, punch your own duplex, okay? I'll have to pay for this."

"I'll pay," I say stubbornly, and Harley steps a bit closer, wrapping the gauze around my hand and putting a piece of tape there to keep it.

"There," she says, as if satisfied, and I look down. Blood is staining the outside of the gauze, but it seems to be slowing down.

"I don't want to say thank you, either," I say, knowing I sound childish but unable to help myself.

Harley laughs, and the sound is like a melody to my ears. It's been a long time since I've heard it.

"You're welcome, anyway." She pats my arm and takes a step back, worrying her bottom lip between her teeth. "Last night-"

"A mistake. I know. You made that crystal clear this morning."

Harley nods slowly. "So, then, you should go back to your place."

I'm still standing in the kitchen and she's so close, just a few steps and I could close the distance, pull her into my arms. Something inside me pulls me toward her and I sway forward a bit from the force of it.

Finally, I turn on my heel and leave, closing the door softly behind me.

Chapter 8

Harley

I have got to find something to keep my mind off Axel fucking Jermaine. Him living just a few hundred feet from me notwithstanding, I'm thinking about him all the time. Especially after last night. I kicked him out this morning because I didn't want this to become a regular thing.

Now, he's trying to kiss me again, moments after I'd seen him with someone else? Not likely. He says that it's work, but what kind of work requires a woman to be that up close and personal?

I sigh, sitting down at the kitchen counter. I suppose that it could have been work, something to do with music. Maybe I reacted too quickly. Nevertheless, I don't want anything to do with him, for my baby's sake, I can't, so I need to stop him from coming in my house again. My baby needs a steady home and a routine. He will bring none of that. His schedules are crazy, he is never here, and I won't be able to rely on him for anything, so I might as well go at it solo and save her from the heartache I went through when I realized we will always be last on his priority list.

I gave in way too quickly when I realized he was hurt, and I need to get my head on straight again. I think maybe a hot bath might help, so I run myself one and remove my clothes, running my fingers over the marks that Axel left on my neck.

I look in the mirror, biting my bottom lip. I hate that I find all those marks so attractive. Axel has always been the possessive type, and it seems like it's just tenfold now that I'm pregnant. After all, he thinks it's someone else's kid. That's what he's going to continue to think, if I have anything to say about it.

For as much as I wanted the happy family with him, I love him too much to keep him on a leash, but I also love this baby too much to have her going through life thinking she doesn't deserve being a priority. Axel's priorities were clear from the start, and it was my mistake that I thought he loved me enough to change them. To put me first once in a while. It's sad really, that I don't love me enough to have demanded it from the start. To have asked him to compromise. But it is too late for us now. That being said, it is not too late to save my baby from the hurt I went through, so I'm doing this for her. Because she is worth it being the center of someone's life, even if it is just mine. She'll never know the neglect and abandonment I felt when I asked him to come home after a show and he always said no, that he would be staying to mingle with the guys and the fans. Not once did he choose me, so why would he choose the baby?

He is happy with his fans, as he always was, and the baby and I will always have each other, and I will always put her first.

I slide naked into the water, running my hands over my belly. The baby kicks until the water rises up, and then she calms down. I really need to schedule a new ultrasound, and I make a mental note to do that in the morning. I take in a deep breath, trying to calm myself down.

I'd pulled into the driveway and seen someone else's car there, and I'd just lost it. I had a feeling that it was a woman, since I didn't recognize the car. Locke, Samuel, and Jackson all had vehicles that I'd recognize, so I swung into the garage like a bat out of hell.

I giggle to myself. I probably gave that girl a hell of a fright. Good. Maybe she won't come back around here anymore. I can't deny that I'm just as possessive as Axel, in my own way.

I trust Axel, but I don't trust his lady fans, that's for sure. I know that Gemma must feel the same way, now that she's with Locke, even though I don't talk to her anymore. I know what type of woman she is, though, and I'm sure she only stays with Locke because she's their manager and she can keep a close eye on him.

I sigh. I miss my friends. I even miss the band members to some degree, especially Samuel. He was always a friend to me, and I kind of regret that I was out the night the band came over to play. I've been so isolated from all my friends in my hometown that I feel lonely most of the time.

Maybe I should look some of them up. Maybe that would keep me from breaking the next time Axel found an excuse to come over. I remember how he kissed me, how he pressed me against the brick, and my skin heats up, feeling hotter than the water swirling around my body.

I slide my hands up to cup my breasts, gasping at the sensations. My sex drive seems to have rocketed up since I reached my second trimester and hasn't gone down since, and yet I have no one to help me with it. No one, that is, except Axel.

I moan as my thumb brushes across my nipple. I

squeeze it more gently than he would, can't quite get my fingers deep enough. I just end up feeling frustrated and hot, and I stand up out of the bath water, still dripping. Once I'm dressed in a maternity nightie, I peek out of the blinds to see that Axel's motorcycle is still in the garage.

My eyes find the box he'd been looking through, the bottle of tequila still sitting open and half empty beside it. I'd put all of those albums out there because they were too painful to look at. I can't deal with the way my heart aches when I look at our wedding photos or watch the video. I wonder if he even knows that it's in there. Remembering what was and imagining what could have been hurt too much, so I had just put them away to see if it would help me heal. It hadn't. Not really.

As I watch, Axel comes out of his duplex and I gasp and back away from the window. I slip the blinds closed but can't help my curiosity and look out again.

Axel takes the bottle of tequila, and after a moment, returns to pick up the box of our wedding mementos and brings it inside his duplex.

I take a deep breath, my heart aching. I have to talk to my mother. That will make things easier.

I call her, and it rings for so long that I'm worried she's not going to pick up.

"Harley? Is it the baby?" She sounds out of breath.

"Oh, God, no, Mom, I've still got a month left," I assure her, and she lets out a long breath.

"You scared me. I was on the elliptical."

That explains the heavy breathing. My mother has always been obsessed with fitness and had tried to pass that habit onto me too, though I wasn't all that fitness-crazy, I had inherited her curves and I stayed in pretty good shape. I enjoy a workout here and there. It certainly takes my mind off things, but my doctor recommended no heavy cardio in the last trimester.

"Everything's okay. I just...needed to talk," I explain hesitantly.

"Is something wrong, honey?" My mother's soft voice makes tears spring to my eyes.

"Everything seems wrong, Mom," I sob, and my mother makes a noise in the back of her throat.

"Oh, honey. Everything's going to be okay. I know the hormones are making you emotional, and you feel all alone right now. But you have me and your father. We're always going to be here for you." My mother's words comfort me, but only a little.

"Can I come over and spend the night with you?" I ask, and my mother chuckles.

"Of course you can, baby. Your dad is on one of his business trips, but he should be here to see you off in the morning."

"Thank you, Mom," I say gratefully, and Mom makes a non-committal sound in the back of her throat.

"Everything's going to be okay, Harley. You'll see."

I hang up the phone and pack myself a quick overnight bag before heading to the garage. Thankfully, Axel is nowhere in sight.

I'm still sniffling when I turn over the key to start the engine, and there's a huge clacking sound before it refuses to start.

"No, don't do this to me," I plead to the car. Axel had bought me this Beetle for our first wedding anniversary. It's been my daily drive ever since, and I've always loved it. All I want is a hug from my mother, and now my car won't start.

The tears come before I even realize I'm sobbing, everything crashing down on my shoulders suddenly, and I lean over the steering wheel and sob.

I could schedule an Uber, or call my mother to come pick me up, but I just feel so defeated that I cry in the car for a while before going back inside. I text my mother that I'm not coming until tomorrow, assuring her that I'm okay even though I feel far from it.

I plop on my bed, exhausted from all the emotions I've been fighting, and slip into a dreamless sleep.

Chapter 9

Axel

I don't sleep, and the sun streaming through my window stabs into my exhausted eyeballs. I didn't pick up the tequila, so that's a plus, at least. I really wanted to, but it'd been sitting out in the garage all night and was probably full of fruit flies. I hadn't had the energy to go to the liquor store, and I polished off the case of beer I'd bought for the band the night before last.

I groan and go to close the blinds, which I'd left open, and see Harley waddling out of the garage into the driveway. She pauses while looking at her yellow Beetle and kicks the tire. I squint, my eyes feeling heavy and my vision fuzzy from lack of sleep.

A man, tall and dressed in a suit, meets her at the driveway, taking her hands in his and squeezing them. I can't see her face clearly to see if she's smiling at him, but I'm sure that she is.

Who the hell is *this* asshole? I think about storming out and asking if this is the coward father of her baby, but I think better of it. She'd all but kicked me out the night we hooked up, and the next day hadn't gone much better.

He opens the car door for her, and I grit my teeth. It makes me want to scream, seeing her slide into his slick silver sedan. I don't know what's going on with her Beetle, but if she needed a ride to work, I could have taken her. Hell, I still have her pink helmet sitting in a box in the duplex. Why hadn't she asked me?

I could stand here and worry about what Harley is up to all day, but I have a meeting with Gemma about the social media schedule. She's probably going to scold me for missing a couple of weeks while I was moving in. I look down at my phone and she's sent me a text message to meet her at the new diner. That's a popular place in this city, I suppose.

Locke and Gemma live about forty-five minutes out, but I guess she's coming in to meet me personally. She must really be mad.

I let out a long breath, snapping the blinds closed as Harley and her mystery man pull out of the driveway. I manage to find a clean pair of jeans and a black t-shirt, and I decide that's good enough for a meeting with the Jack and the Spades' manager.

Gemma's a great manager, but she has a sharp tongue, and I expect to feel its wrath today. Gemma's been sleep deprived from the pregnancy, or so they say, and she's been in a mood every time we've met up. I wonder if Harley is suffering too, but soon shut that off. I can't think about her now.

When I take the motorcycle to the diner and walk in, though, Gemma seems almost...glowing.

I give her a look as I slide into the booth. "You're looking good."

Gemma beams. "Thank you."

"You're glowing. If that baby had popped yet, I'd guess

you were pregnant again," Gemma stares at me for a long moment. "That's a funny way to say I've looked like shit for the past three weeks."

I groan. "Come on, Gemma, that's not what I meant."

Gemma laughs. "Nah, I know I've haven't been my best lately. Cain has been kicking like crazy, and he never sleeps. And if he doesn't sleep, I don't sleep."

I wince. Poor Gemma. Again I find myself wondering if Harley is going through the same.

"But I finally got a full night's sleep last night, thus I look hot." She grins at me.

"You always look hot," I grin back, knowing that Locke would hit me for that comment. Oh well. I am who I am.

"Thanks, Axel," Gemma takes a big gulp of her latte. "Now, we need to talk."

I gulp. "Am I in trouble?"

Gemma sighs. "No, of course not. I know you were moving into a new place, so I'm not going to get on your ass about missing a couple of weeks doing your TikToks. It's your income stream, after all."

"Minus your fifteen percent," I drawl, and Gemma rolls her eyes.

"Minus The *Spades'* fifteen percent. It all goes back into the band." She ticks off with her fingers while she makes a list. "Marketing, equipment, venues, taxes..."

"I know, I know. I'm getting a great deal," I respond, repeating her words to me when we first drew up the contract. Gemma does a great job keeping up with the self-employment taxes and all the legal stuff, so I don't complain about any money she takes off the top. Hell, after all, she was able to finance our whole national tour with just cover charges, so in my opinion she works miracles.

"I wanted to talk to you because Locke told me that you moved into a duplex with Harley."

Shit. I shouldn't have run my mouth off at garage practice. I should have known Locke would spill everything to his new wife. Traitor.

"I didn't move in *with* Harley. I just happened to move in next to her."

Gemma arches a well-groomed eyebrow. "You're trying to tell me you couldn't find anywhere else to stay but next to your ex-wife?"

I open my mouth but then shut it again, not having a good response. It doesn't matter, because Gemma isn't finished.

"Your ex-wife who you're still very much in love with," she continues, and I bang my head lightly on the table as the server comes over.

The server looks at me curiously but doesn't comment, thank God. I order the home fries and a bacon cheeseburger while Gemma orders hashbrowns and the prime rib sandwich.

"I didn't know that she was staying there until the papers were signed," I lied, and Gemma raises an eyebrow again.

"You're lying," she says simply, drinking more of her latte, and I let out a long sigh.

"Fine. I'm lying. I saw her when I toured the place, and I don't know, I thought..." I trail off. I'm not sure what I thought. Maybe that I could annoy Harley into getting back together with me? I guess that'd been my hope, that she'd see me every day and eventually realize that we were meant to be together, despite the baby in her belly.

"You thought what? That she'd fall back into your arms?" Gemma scoffs.

My heart sinks a little. I feel stupid, like it's ridiculous to think that way, but part of me did. Part of me still does.

"You never know," I mumble, tearing apart the straw for my water with my hands. My stomach rumbles again, the smells of the diner making hunger gnaw at me.

"Are you sleeping?" she asks me, looking at me shrewdly, and I feel like it's pointless to lie.

"Not much," I admit, and Gemma makes a tsking sound in the back of her throat.

"Drinking too much, not eating or sleeping enough....you're starting to sound like Jackson a couple of years ago," Gemma warns.

I bang my head on the table once more before lifting my head, the Formica stinging my forehead enough to bring things back into focus again. I find that being exhausted is almost worse than being drunk in terms of keeping my wits about me.

"I know. I'm going to do better," I promise, and desperately try to change the subject. "What do you think about the new TikTok? Sophie?"

Gemma shrugs. "She's cute. Got a good voice." She looks at me again with those shrewd eyes of hers. "Are you fucking her?"

This time, I'm the one that chokes, on air instead of water since I hadn't even been drinking anything. I know that Gemma doesn't pull any punches, but I wasn't expecting her to be that blunt.

"So what if I was?" I ask, and Gemma bites at her lower lip, a nervous habit.

"I know that I'm not the best person to be saying this, but shitting where you eat isn't always the right move." Gemma has a point there, even though she is married to our drummer. "Especially if it's just a fling to get back at Harley for being pregnant."

"Locke told you that, too, huh?" I ask, only a little bitter. I know that Locke doesn't keep secrets from his wife, and even if he hadn't told her, Jackson would have.

"How are you, Axel? Really?" Gemma reaches across the table to touch my arm and I soften at the gesture.

Gemma had been my best friend on tour other than the guys, and I'd been able to reveal a lot to her that I wouldn't to the men that I consider my brothers. I can't lie to her, no matter how much I might want to avoid the situation.

"I'm...I'm not great," I manage, my voice sounding hoarse from lack of sleep. "I can't stop thinking about how some asshole got her pregnant, about how she might still be seeing him now."

"You're divorced, Axel," Gemma says gently, squeezing my forearm. "You have to let her go."

I look at her for a moment, my brow furrowed. "How do I do that, Gem?" I ask, and I sound almost desperate. I *am* desperate, desperate to feel any other way than awful about what's going on with me and Harley right now.

Gemma sighs. "I can't tell you that, bubs. Have you told her how you feel?"

"Only about a hundred times," I mutter, even though I'm not sure I really have. I've begged for her to come back. I've told her that I missed her. Hell, I'd even told her that I'd change even though I wasn't sure that I would. I've always been faithful to her, hell, even *after* we were divorced, but I can't imagine giving up music, which I guess is what she wants.

"Then there's nothing else you can do. You have to let it go." Gemma pauses as the food comes, picking a ranch and bacon drenched fry off the plate. "And you need to get the hell out of that duplex."

She pops the fry into her mouth and that's it, advice over. I have no idea how the hell to go about letting go of Harley Telman. She's been my north star for as long as I can remember, the one thing that I reach for, other than my music. I thought that she was supportive of me in that, too.

After all, it was how we had first bonded.

"Green Day," she said, licking the lollipop that I'd watched her steal from the corner store. "Don't you think they're a little over-rated?"

"American Idiot is the punk rock anthem of our generation," I said earnestly, and Harley giggled, a sound that seemed to light up the dark alley we were standing in.

"I think so too." She leaned in closer, as if she were telling me a secret. "Just don't tell my friends I said that. They're into Maroon Five, now."

"Bunch of try-hards," I scoffed, and Harley giggled again, nodding her head. I watched her for a moment, the line of her jaw, the way her chin turned up just slightly, as if she were defiant. I wanted her so much that it hurt somewhere deep in my bones. "I play guitar," I told her, hoping that it would grease the wheels, and her blue eyes lit up.

"Oh yeah? Can you play any Audioslave?"

That was it, the moment I'd been lost. She was the star pointing north and I just followed.

I shake my head, trying to rid myself of the memories.

"I have to let her go," I repeat, and Gemma nods sympathetically with a mouth full of home fries.

I look down at my food, and suddenly, I'm not hungry at all.

Chapter 10

Harley

After my mini-breakdown last night, I texted my work group chat to tell them that I'd be a little late for work, given that my car was broken down. A few minutes later, Roland had texted me privately:

Do you need a ride to work in the morning?

I'm grateful for the offer, because I'm stressed out and can't imagine dealing with a tow truck and an Uber first thing in the morning. I don't think much about saying yes. After all, Roland has never pushed about us being more, though he has stated the possibility is there, he says he wants us to be more but is happy being my friend until I'm ready. I can only wonder if I'll ever be.

I kick the tire of my stupid car as I walk by, and Roland chuckles, taking my hands in his. I must have had tears in my eyes, because he squeezes my hands comfortingly. It's nice that he opens the car door for me. That's not really something I'm used to, since before I was used to riding on the back of Axel's motorcycle and now I just pretty much drive myself.

"Thank you for coming to pick me up," I tell him, and he waves his hands dismissively.

"No problem. You're on my way, anyway."

I raise an eyebrow because I'm pretty sure he lives about half an hour away from me, but I don't comment. He's being nice, and I don't want to ruin it by asking questions.

I blow my bangs out of my face, sweating a little. I'm always hot since I've gotten pregnant, and he doesn't have the air on.

As if he senses my discomfort, he turns on the air full blast and I sigh, the breeze making me feel ten times better.

"How is everything going with the baby? Healthy?" he asks, and I wince.

"I've got an appointment coming up," I lie, even though I have yet to schedule my appointment. I reminded myself yet again to schedule that on my lunch break.

It isn't like I'm not worried about the baby. At my twenty-week appointment, everything had been perfect. The baby is healthy, even though I don't yet know the sex, and the doctor told me that I'd likely carry her to term or even beyond, since this is my first baby.

Roland nods. "I see you have a new neighbor."

I stare at him for a moment before I remember that he was the only coworker to take me up on my offer to cook for them if they helped me move, and that's why he'd known where I lived and that I used to live alone.

"Don't get me started," I mutter, and Roland laughs.

"Not the world's best neighbor, I'm guessing? I saw the motorcycle. The engines on those are so annoying."

I don't agree, since the sound of a motorcycle engine spikes my adrenaline and makes me feel excited, so I just hum in the back of my throat.

Roland doesn't keep talking about my neighbor, thank

God, changing the subject to talk about work, and I'm grateful for it.

Work itself goes by quickly and quietly enough, nothing of note happening. I remembered to schedule my doctor's appointment at lunch and when Roland offers me a ride home at five, I accept.

"Would you like to get something to eat on the way?" he asks, and I shake my head.

"Not today. I'm not feeling so well." That isn't a lie, I have been feeling off ever since last night when the Beetle wouldn't start. It doesn't escape me that The Beetle is the one thing I still have from our marriage that isn't boxed up in the garage, and now it's shot to shit. Just like my marriage to Axel.

I guess that's why I'm feeling so depressed about it. That isn't exactly something that I can tell Roland, though, without giving him what amounts to my whole life story. I'm quiet on the drive home, and Roland clears his throat when he pulls up in the drive, looking over at me.

Axel's motorcycle is parked in the garage, but he must be inside. I let out a relieved breath.

"Harley," Roland starts, waiting to continue until I look at him. "I'd like to take you out sometime soon."

I blink at him. "What?"

What happened to being happy just being my friend until I'm ready? In another lifetime, this might be a welcome overture. Roland is handsome and sweet as can be, but I'm just not in the right frame of mind to go out on a date, especially not now. Not while I'm so pregnant. Not with Axel so... here.

"You know I like you and I'd like to show you how great we could be," Roland says softly, and I begin to feel bad that I'm going to turn him down.

"Roland, I'm sorry," I start, and Roland smiles weakly, looking away.

"That's what I thought you were going to say."

"It's just...it's not a good time for me...." I gesture to my stomach, even though that's not the only reason it isn't a good time.

"I don't care about that," Roland insists. "I love kids."

I let out a little laugh, I can't help it, but not because I'm making fun of him. I just find it cute.

"I *am* sorry, Roland," I tell him earnestly, and he gives me another smile, stronger this time.

"Maybe someday the timing won't be off," he says hopefully, and I smile back sadly.

"Maybe," I answer, even though I'm positive that I'll never be in the right place to date someone like Roland. And not because he has any problem or flaw. No. I should be so happy getting such a nice guy.

I just don't think I'll ever be over Axel Jermaine.

* * *

I cook myself some salmon, rice, and vegetables and everything goes well until I start to wash up the dishes from dinner. The pipes groan, which isn't unusual, but then the water won't come out of the faucet.

Irritated, I turn off the water and turn it back on. The second I do, the faucet (which had admittedly been a little wobbly since I moved in), falls off and water sprays all over my face and chest.

I can't help myself, the cold water makes me scream shrilly, and the next thing I know someone's banging on my door. There are tears springing to the backs of my eyes from the shock and frustration. Fucking *hormones*.

"I'm okay!" I yell, but Axel pounds on the door again, probably unable to hear me over the spray of the water.

When I let him in, his eyes look wild until he surveys the room and the water pooling on the floor.

"Oh, shit," he mumbles, and a hysterical laugh starts to bubble in the back of my throat. I manage to keep it down and sit at the counter, defeated. I have no idea how to shut the water off or what's wrong with the pipe.

I don't want to ask Axel to do it, so I'm grateful when he climbs below the sink to turn the valve off, water beading on his face and neck when he stands back up.

"I can handle it," I tell him, and he gives me a look like I'm crazy.

"You're about to pop that baby out any moment and you're standing ankle deep in water, Harley. Let me help you."

"I'll call a plumber," I say stubbornly.

"Call the baby's father," Axel mumbles, and anger heats up my blood.

"What the hell is that supposed to mean?"

Axel straightens up from where he'd been looking under the sink and he gestures to the room and then points at the half-finished crib in the living room.

"You're doing all this by yourself, Harley!" His voice rises. "Where the hell is he? Who's taking care of you?"

I stand up, nearly knocking over the barstool with my clumsy pregnant body.

"I can take care of myself. I took care of myself all those nights you didn't come home, or don't you remember?"

Axel advances toward me but I don't back down, raising my chin up and frowning up at him.

"I remember everything, Harley. Every moment that I

spent with you," he says in a low voice, and I swallow hard, fighting tears all over again.

"And every moment that you didn't?" I respond softly, and Axel winces as if I'd hit him.

"I don't want to spend another moment without you," Axel tells me, and it's the same old story. It's the same old song and dance we've been doing for years, but somehow, it still works. In the back of my head, I know this is what I want. I want Axel and this baby, for us to be a family.

I lean toward him, unable to help myself, and he sweeps me into his arms. My belly bounces against his but he doesn't seem to care, leaning down to kiss me deep and thoroughly.

My arms go around his neck, and I'm lost all over again to Axel, the man I'll never get over.

Chapter 11

Axel

Harley feels the same in my arms as she ever did, except for the swell of her belly against mine. I'd been angry when she'd been so stubborn, but it was like anger went right to lust with Harley. That's the way it's always been.

We always make love after we fight, and it doesn't seem like much has changed since we divorced. Not much except for her swollen belly, that is.

It still makes jealousy boil in my blood, makes me want to ask a dozen questions about who he is, how it happened, why he isn't still around. But I know that the more questions I ask, the more likely she is to kick me out.

"You drive me *crazy*," I tell Harley, another rerun, something I'd said to her a hundred times. I kiss along her collarbone and on the marks I left on her throat, tugging down the turtleneck she is still wearing from work. "I don't want you to hide these. I want everyone to know you're mine."

"I belong to myself," Harley says stubbornly, and that's

a repeat, too, something she often said in response to my possessiveness.

"I belong to you," I say earnestly, kissing her pouting mouth again, and the furrow of her brow starts to smooth out as she melts into me.

"What about that girl?" Harley asks me, and I honestly have no idea who she's talking about.

"What girl?" I murmur, kissing below her ear before nipping at her earlobe, but Harley puts both small hands on my chest to push me away, more gently now than the last time.

"The girl who was here in the garage," Harley manages, sounding like she is speaking through gritted teeth. I hold back a grin.

I love it when Harley is as possessive as I am, which is often. She's always been jealous of my fans, and to be honest, sometimes I played it up to rile her.

"It's just for work," I say honestly, not blinking as I stare down at her and Harley narrows her eyes. I'm telling the truth. I have no interest in Sophie beyond her singing, and I made that clear to her.

"She sure was sitting close to you," she mutters, and I laugh this time, I can't help it.

It feels like something's changing and I hope it's changing for the better, hope that Harley comes to her senses, realizes that we can work through this. I'm still angry about the baby and I know that will be something we need to work through, but I can work through anything, if I've got Harley by my side.

"What about that jerk who came to pick you up this morning?" I ask her, more teasing than actually angry. If he'd been the baby's father, I assumed he would have come inside after he dropped her off.

"He's a friend," she says, but I don't like the way she looks away from me. I take her jaw in my hand, squeezing to make her mouth pop open and she lets out a moan in the back of her throat.

As feisty as Harley is, she loves it when I take control, when I manhandle her, and it seems like that hasn't changed, either.

I cover her mouth with my own, sticking my tongue to slide alongside hers and nipping at her bottom lip, hard enough to get her attention.

"Axel," she moans, and God, I love the way my name sounds on her lips.

"Tell me you want me," I command. I want to say: *"Tell me you love me,"* but I know that will scare her off, make her push me away.

"I want you. Want you right now, Axel, I can't wait." She bunches her A-line skirt over her hips, turns to bend over the barstool, holding her forearms over it instead of draping her body over it to protect her belly.

I groan low in my throat and take off her panties, not a particularly sexy pair but the way her thigh-highs wrap around her thick flesh makes my cock plump in my jeans. I love Harley's curves, can never seem to find any other women with her figure. I can't help but bite gently at the curve of her ass as I stand up from removing her panties.

I roll my hips against her, still in my jeans but rubbing my clothed erection against her bare sex. Harley rocks back against me, turning her head to kiss me sloppily. I kiss her back eagerly, moaning into her mouth as I rock up against her again. She's so slick against me she might stain my jeans, but I don't care.

I unbutton them and push them down, releasing myself with a hiss before wrapping one hand around myself, guiding myself inside her. She's always so *slick*, so wet that I can slide right in.

"You fit me like a glove, you know that? You always have," I growl right up against her ear, thrusting up the way I know she likes and she cries out, putting her head down.

I wrap my hand around her blonde hair, pull her head up. "Want to hear you, sweetheart," I croon, and she grunts before crying out again when I thrust into her harder.

My balls are drawing up already as she clenches around me in a vice, and I know she's close to coming so I grit my teeth and keep going, my hips moving faster with losing rhythm as I get closer myself.

My mouth often runs away with me when I'm buried inside Harley, and nothing's changed there, either, it turns out.

"I love you," I moan against her ear, holding her up with my forearm just under her breasts and she's up on her tip toes as I thrust up into her but the angle is just right. She whispers my name over and over when she comes, tightening around me, and I spill inside of her with a shout.

When I start to come down, my ears heat up as I realize what I said. I wait for her to push me away, wait for her to kick me out and when she doesn't, panting, anxiety rises up in me just waiting for it.

She turns to me and opens her mouth, and I shake my head, pulling out of her slowly and zipping my jeans up.

"I know," I say, softly and a little bitterly. "I know you want me to go."

Harley's mouth snaps close and she gives me a barely perceptible nod that makes my heart drop to somewhere around my toes.

I can't look at her as I walk out and storm back toward

my duplex. This time, I don't ignore the fresh bottle of tequila on my counter.

I'm only human, after all.

Chapter 12

Harley

For the first time since he's moved in, I honestly want Axel to stay, but when he pulls out of me, tells me that he knows I want him to go, I just nod. If he wanted to stay, he would have, right?

If he wanted to, he would, my friend Greta always told me in high school. It's a sentiment I've thought about many times. It doesn't matter what Axel says if he never changes, and that's what I hold onto as he walks out the door, closing it softly behind him.

I have to stop doing this. My heart aches and tears burn at the backs of my eyes as I go to the bedroom, telling myself that I'll clean up the mess of the kitchen in the morning. It's Friday, so I don't have to go to work in the morning, and I don't need Axel to help me.

Do I want Axel, though? Still? After all this time?

Yes, something in the back of my head says. *You'll always want him.* But regardless of what I want, I can't think of just me anymore. I have someone else who will depend on me to make the right decisions soon enough, and him staying would definitely be the wrong decision.

My biggest fear, other than something happening to the life growing inside me, is Axel finding out that the baby is his. It isn't as if I think he'll be a terrible father. Far from it. In fact, Axel's good around kids. He would be an amazing father. But the problem is, if Axel knows this baby is his, he'll never give up on us. He'll want us to be a family no matter what, and it won't matter if he really wants us or not. He'll settle down because he *has* to, not because he wants to. I want him to want us, and not just because his baby is growing in my belly. I want him to choose *us*.

When we were together, all I ever wanted was for him to find a balance in which he would choose to be with me at least once in a while. But when asked to choose, I was never the answer. He had his nightlife and he never once decided to come home early just to be able to spend time with me. The fans were more important. And I get that he has to, because of his career, but could he not choose to be just the two of us once in a while?

A baby might make him settle down, but it wouldn't mean he is choosing us because he wants to. Only because he felt some kind of obligation. I don't want him like that. I'd never do that to him. Clip his wings like that. I'd rather let him go. Just like I did before.

And no matter how much I try to tell myself that I don't want him in any case, I know that's a lie. I tug off my clothes and lie down on my side on my bed, not even bothering to wash off my makeup from work.

After fighting them so many times in the last twenty-four hours, I let the tears come.

* ✦ *

A knocking on my door, softer than Axel's usual pounding, wakes me up, and I throw on a robe to answer the door.

It's Axel, surprisingly, holding a toolbox in one hand and a new faucet in the other. He pushes past me into the duplex before I can stop him.

"Please don't argue with me, Harley. I'm fixing your sink." He looks around at the floor, which is still pooled with water, and he goes to the linen closet to grab some towels, lying them over the mess.

I worry my bottom lip between my teeth, a bad habit, especially since I tend to bite it pretty hard. "You don't have to do this," I insist, and Axel gives me a hard look.

"Is your baby daddy going to come over and do it? Because I haven't seen him around here." he snaps, and I roll my eyes, turning away from him.

I want to tell him my baby daddy is doing it right now, but I can never reveal that secret. Some part of me wants to yell at him, tell him that it's his fault that I can't go out with anyone else, that he's ruined me for all other men somehow. But I can't. Even though he'd probably like that too much.

"I could have done it myself," I grumbled, and Axel barks out a laugh.

"Sweetheart, you don't have a handy bone in your body and you know that I know that."

I huff. He's right, but he didn't have to *say* it. I'm clumsy and don't know a Phillips screwdriver from a flathead, if I'm honest. My father or Axel had always taken care of everything.

Axel slides under the sink and starts to bang around in there, and he calls to me to keep the conversation going.

"What happened to the Beetle?"

I'm surprised he hasn't already asked me that, given that he bought me the car for our first wedding anniversary.

74

"I don't know. It just wouldn't start."

Axel grunts. "I'll take a look at it after I'm done here."

I don't know how to tell him not to, and I really do need the help. I have a little nest egg saved for the baby, but I don't want to dip into that to get the Beetle fixed.

"Thank you," I say softly, and Axel peeks his head from under the sink.

"What was that?" he asks, grinning, and I shake my head.

"Never mind," I mumble, and he chuckles low in his throat.

Axel gets the faucet fitted in no time, and he sits up, brushing his hands as if telling me he was done.

He stands up and turns on the cold water, and then the hot. It doesn't go spraying all over him. Traitor faucet.

"Look, I appreciate your help, let me give you some money for it," I tell him, picking up my purse, and Axel frowns at me, looking offended.

"You don't have to *pay* me, Harley. I'm your neighbor."

"Is that why you're doing all this? Being a good neighbor?" I ask suspiciously, and he takes a couple of steps toward me.

"What do you think, Harley? Why am I doing all this? Why am I helping you?"

I swallow, having not expected him to ask me so point blank.

"I don't know," I say softly, looking away, and Axel snorts.

"No, I guess you wouldn't."

He storms outside to the car, popping the hood. I meekly took the keys out to him, knowing that he's angry and not wanting to make it worse.

"Axel," I tell him as he reaches down into the car.

75

He grunts in response.

"Axel, I'm sorry," I say, my voice a little louder, and his blue eyes shoot up to mine.

"It's okay," he says, his face softening, and he favors me with a smile. "Just let me help you, okay?"

I nod slowly, unsure why tears are filling my eyes. I look away and discreetly wipe them, standing around for a bit to see if I can help.

I lie down on the couch after an hour when he's still not finished, and as I'm dozing, I hear his motorcycle take off, presumably to get more parts from the store.

"Harley," someone murmurs my name and I slowly open my eyes to see Axel sitting next to me on the couch. The curtains are drawn, the room dark.

"Axel?" I call, confused, and he strokes my cheek, brushing a piece of hair from my face.

"The Beetle's up and running," he tells me, and I grin.

"Really?" I sit up. "Thank you, Axel." I look up at him, biting my bottom lip again.

My legs spread when he puts a hand on my thigh.

"This doesn't mean anything, you know," I say, although that fact is seeming less and less true every day.

Axel's eyes shoot to mine and I can see the hurt in them. He looks wide open, raw in a way that he hasn't been since we'd moved into this duplex.

It makes my heart ache, seeing the hurt on his face, knowing it mirrors mine perfectly.

"I know that. I'll take anything I can get," Axel murmurs, trailing his hand up my thigh, my robe falling open.

I swallow hard, knowing that I should stop him but he parts my lower lips with one hand, looks down at me.

"So pink and pretty," he praises, and he kneels down on the floor, looping my knees around his shoulders.

He tugs my legs to get me closer, so that my sex is right up in his face, and he buries his face in me, his mouth latching around my clit.

"Oh, fuck, *Axel,*" I moan loudly, and I swear I can feel him grin against me. He loves the way I moan his name in bed. He always has, and seems like nothing has changed.

The way my body reacts to him doesn't change, either, I'm sitting up on the couch and trying to see over my belly as he sucks my clit, sliding one finger, then two, inside me. When I gasp out his name, Axel lifts his head and I pout.

"Don't stop," I plead, and this time he does grin at me, openly, the lower half of his mouth covered in my slick.

He pumps his fingers in and out of me until he adds a third and he plants a kiss on my inner thigh, moaning against my skin.

"Told myself I'd eat you out all night, wait until your thighs were shaking," he murmurs. Pleasure shoots up my spine and I arch my back as he angles his fingers up in a "come hither" motion. "But all I can think about is being inside you."

"It won't.....it won't work from this angle," I manage, and Axel hums, looking at the swell of my pregnant belly with something like bitterness.

Then he removes his fingers from me and pulls me up on shaking legs.

"Then I'll bend you over the couch arm," he says simply, always the problem solver, and I let out a giddy laugh.

I feel almost lightheaded with lust like so many times before with Axel. He's like a drug to me, one I'm addicted to and I just can't stop at one.

Axel presses gently on my lower back and I drape myself over the couch arm, making sure my belly is on the inside of the couch and not split by the couch arm.

He doesn't enter me right away, and I whine, turning around to look at him. He spreads my cheeks apart, looking down at me hungrily, before he makes a sound in the back of his throat.

The sight of his hunger for me makes me moan so loudly that I press my mouth against my forearm to stop the sound and Axel wraps his fist around my hair, tugging, and not gently.

He pushes himself into me while he twists my face around to look at him.

"Don't you hide your sounds from me, sweetheart. Want to know I'm doing a good job."

"Fuck, Axel, you know you are," I gasp, rolling my hips back against him when he stubbornly refuses to move. "You fuck me so good."

"Is that right?" he drawls, and slowly begins to move, not fast enough, not *hard* enough and I let out a frustrated breath. "I know how you like it, Harls. Hard and fast and rough. But tonight, I'm going to take my time with you."

He moves his hips into me slow and steady, hard like I like but slower than the pace that can get me off quickly, and I let out a low whine.

"Axel," I gasp, pleading with him, but he doesn't speed up. This isn't like him. Axel usually likes to get me off as quickly as possible, and he's good at it. He knows just where to touch me, just how to angle so that I come hard and fast, but this time it's like a slow build at the bottom of my stomach. It reminds me of when we first started dating and he would eat me out for an hour before he ever entered me.

Axel grips onto my hips so that I can't roll back against him.

"You're not going to tease me into going faster, sweetheart. I only get a little time with you, so I'm going to take advantage," he murmurs, and I'm not sure what he means but it feels good, how he's slowly pushing into me, almost pulling out and ramming back into me hard but with a steady rhythm. I'm close before I realize it, after only a few thrusts, and I blame it on being worked up from all the pregnancy hormones.

"I'm close," I whisper, and then I groan when Axel tugs my head back up from where I'd been hanging over the couch.

"What was that? I couldn't hear you," he drawls, and I know he's got a smug grin on his face.

"I'm close, I'm close," I say louder, and Axel keeps his pace, achingly slow, but it doesn't matter, I'm tumbling over the edge of my orgasm and crying out his name in just a few more thrusts.

Now, Axel will speed up, give me what I want and vault me into another orgasm. Despite what I think, though, he doesn't, still pressing against my walls slow and steady.

"Oh fuck," I manage, and Axel chuckles low in his throat.

"I told you I was going to take my time with you. Want to make this last," he pants. His breathing is getting shorter, and I can tell that he's close to the edge, so I purposely clench my inner muscles around him.

"C'mon, baby. Come inside me. Fill me up," I say throatily, knowing that's what he likes to hear, and Axel groans loud in the back of his throat.

"Should have thought to gag you. Forgot what a filthy mouth you have," he murmurs, and I can't help but grin.

"You love my filthy mouth," I say, not thinking about the words that are coming out of my mouth, and Axel goes silent for a moment, his hips stuttering before he resumes his slow pace.

"I do," he admits, doubling over me to kiss my neck, nipping there so that there will be a small line of his teeth later. "I love every part of you, you know that?"

Axel hadn't talked like this since we'd started hooking up again, and I frown. I don't want feelings to go along with my lust, so I don't respond. He starts to move faster, and I groan, bracing my hands on the cushion in front of me.

"You look beautiful like this, you know, all spread open for me," he continues, and I'm glad that he has gone back to dirty talk instead of sweet nothings. "All for me."

I don't complain or argue, but Axel tugs at my hair, nonetheless.

"Tell me you want me," he commands, and I swallow hard before I speak.

"I want you. I always want you," I say honestly, and Axel looks at me as if he's not quite satisfied.

"Does anyone else make you feel the way I do?" he asks in a low, dangerous tone, having almost completely stopped his thrusts.

I don't know what he's asking, exactly, but the answer, if I want to be truthful, is the same either way.

"No," I breathe out. "No, no one else, Axel."

"Say my name again," he demands, his fist wrapping tighter in my blonde hair.

"Axel," I say again, louder, and I feel his thrusts speed up, getting sloppier.

"Fuck," he curses. "Wanted this to last. Didn't want this to be over."

I don't know what he means by that, but he drops my

head and begins to fuck me hard and fast, in earnest, and I cry out his name again when I come for a second time.

When I feel him spill inside me, I can hear him breathing hard, nearly doubled over me, kissing along my shoulder. He doesn't pull out and I wince, in an uncomfortable position.

"Let me up," I tell him, and he hesitates.

"I'm not done," he says, but he's softening inside me and I laugh a little.

"We're done for now," I say, and he reluctantly pulls out of me, readjusting his jeans. I flush a little as I stand up on shaky legs, adjusting my skirt.

Axel is staring at me like he wants to say something, and I bite down on my bottom lip, looking away.

"Ask me to stay," he says quietly, and I close my mouth tight, making my lips a thin line. I don't say that I can't ask him to do that, and I don't have to, because he strides out the door, slamming it behind him.

Chapter 13

Axel

As soon as I get back to my duplex, I call up Jackson. Locke is too busy with Gemma to give me what I need, and Samuel is too buttoned up. I need the lead singer of the Spades tonight, and I'm hoping he's available.

Jackson answers the phone after the fourth ring. "Hey, Ax."

"I need to go out tonight," I blurt out, and Jackson laughs, the sound tinny through the phone.

"Need is a pretty strong word."

"Let me rephrase. If I don't replace my blood with tequila in the next few hours, I don't know what I'll do."

Jackson pauses, and I can nearly hear him frowning over the phone line. "Is everything okay, bubs?"

Tears spring to the backs of my eyes but I blink them away. "Sure. Everything's five by five," I say, attempting to sound cheerful. "'I'm just going a little stir-crazy."

I hear shuffling on the line and then Jackson's voice lowers.

"Is it Harley?" he asks in a soft voice, and I squeeze my eyes shut, sighing.

"Isn't it always Harley?" I ask, and Jackson hums.

"Fair enough. You want me to come pick you up?"

"Nah, I'm taking an Uber. Not planning to be sober more than half an hour."

"Shit, okay. I'll get a ride. See you at the Dozen in half an hour."

I chug the rest of the tequila that I had left over, only a couple of shots worth, as I wait for the Uber. The driver tries to make small talk but I'm silent long enough that he gives up.

I get to the Dirty Dozen before Jackson, and I camp out at the bar, ordering two tequila shots. This time, Sophie isn't working, it's some guy named Andrew who seems nice enough. When I take both the tequila shots and ask for another, he raises an eyebrow, but he doesn't say anything, luckily.

I'm only a little drunk when Jackson arrives and I grin at him and throw an arm around his shoulders, sliding him a shot of tequila.

"My best friend!"

"Samuel's your best friend," Jackson says dryly. "I'm just the friend most willing to get fucked up with you."

"That makes you my best friend, this week," I insist. "Everything's on me."

Jackson's mouth is turned down at the corners, which means he's in a *mood*, but that's good for me. When Jackson's in a mood is when he goes off the rails, and I would *love* to go off the rails tonight.

"What's going on?" Jackson asks after the second tequila shot, his shoulders seeming looser than before. "With you and Harley, I mean."

I shrug. "We've been hooking up."

Jackson gapes at me. "You've been *what*?"

I groan. "I know, I know, it's a bad idea. I just can't seem to help myself. I can't keep my hands off her."

"Even though she's knocked up with someone else's kid?"

That stings, and I roll my head around my shoulders. "Even so," I say tersely, and Jackson sighs.

"I'm not trying to be an asshole, Ax. It's just like–where does this go? What are you gonna do if the father comes back into the picture?"

I stiffen. "That's not going to happen. He abandoned her. She won't let him back in."

"You don't know that."

"I know Harley," I insist.

Jackson stares at me. "Do you? Anymore?"

I think about it for a long moment. Things have changed, that's for sure, with her swollen belly and the way she kicks me out every time we hook up. I've only been able to stay the night once, and she pushed me out the door first thing the next morning. Harley doesn't seem to want to get back together, and I know it's a bad idea to keep hooking up with her.

"I don't know," I say softly, and order us another round.

Things begin to go fuzzy around the edges and Sophie comes in for her shift, smiling at me and chatting with Jackson about social media. I'm barely listening, thinking of how Harley writhes up beneath me when I touch her, the sound of my name on her lips. All I ever think about is Harley, lately, and I try to focus my double vision on Sophie. I should get some work done, try to get my mind off things.

"Do you want to take me home?" I ask, words slurred

84

around the edges, and Sophie's eyes widen. I don't tell her that's not what I meant, figuring it doesn't matter. Nothing matters anymore, not without Harley.

Alcohol is a depressant, after all, and it's beginning to do its job on my mood. Everything seems to hang over me in a cloud: Harley's pregnancy, the way she keeps pushing me away.

I barely remember getting home, and when I wake up, there's a pounding on the door to match the pounding in my head.

I groan and make it to the doorway in a stumble, still reeling. I must still be a little drunk, and when I look at my phone it's only six in the morning, meaning I'd only gotten a few thin hours of sleep.

When I open the door, I'm not completely surprised to see Harley standing there, her chin jutted upward, glaring up at me with fire in her blue eyes.

"I asked you for *one* thing, Axel," she said tightly, and I blinked at her, my eyes bleary.

"What?" My voice is hoarse even to my own ears.

"You *know* what, Axel," she says firmly, and to my horror, I realize that tears are welling in her eyes. She wipes at them angrily, turning away from me.

"Harley, honey-" I begin, and her eyes snap to mine.

"Don't you dare call me that. Not now," she hisses, and I inwardly groan. What the hell did I do last night?

"Listen, Harley, I swear I don't know what you're talking about," I try again.

Harley scoffs. "Don't play dumb, Axel. I know you were drunk but you don't black out."

I blink at her. "Maybe I didn't use to black out. I drink a lot more now, sweetheart. Wanna know why?"

Harley huffs out a breath. "Don't turn this around on

me. I had one rule when you moved in here, and you have broken it *twice*."

I think about it for a long moment, the gears in my head turning way too slowly for comfort. The last time she was angry with me was....oh shit. *Sophie.*

I swallow hard. "Uh, if this is about Sophie, it was for work."

"So, she kissed you for *work*?" Harley spits out, and I realize she's not just mad. She's *jealous*. That's rich, coming from her.

I manage to bite back a smile, but it's tough.

"So, you're jealous? That's what all this is about?"

"No!" she nearly yells, and then she looks down at the floor, wiping away more tears. I want to caress her face, brush those tears away with my thumbs, but I think she would hit me if I tried. "I just... I asked you not to bring women here."

Her words are softer on that last sentence, almost sad, and my heart aches.

"Sophie and I aren't anything, Harley. I was shitfaced. I barely remember getting home, so I don't even remember what happened with her. Doesn't that tell you that it's not anything serious?"

"I don't care if it's serious, Axel. I don't want you fucking other women here," she says firmly, and then pauses. "Maybe that's not fair. I don't know."

I feel anger rise up in me, even though she's being shockingly self-aware.

"I pay rent here, Harley. This is my home. I can do whatever I want to within the confines of my duplex."

Harley's eyes shoot to mine again, and this time she doesn't bother wiping away the tears that spill down her cheeks.

"Then keep it out of the garage," she says firmly, and stalks off toward her side of the duplex.

I sigh heavily, stepping after her and stumbling off the front stoop.

"Harley!" I call, but she's getting into a car, the same one that the guy picked her up in last time.

I curse under my breath. How did she expect me to apologize for something I don't even remember? Especially when she won't even let me.

I watch as the guy in the driver's side reaches over to hug her, gritting my teeth, and look away as they pull off.

Who the hell *is* that? If I can't bring girls home, then why is it okay for this asshole to come and pick her up every morning? Is he the father? My blood boils just thinking about it.

Harley Telman-Jermaine has some things to answer for when she gets home.

Chapter 14

Harley

Work goes by in a blur. As much as Roland starts up conversations, I just can't keep track of them. Everything feels fuzzy and off somehow, like I'm in some sort of trance.

I can't stop thinking about how my heart nearly stopped when I saw that woman kissing Axel before pushing him into his duplex. She'd seen me, turned to me, and her eyes widened a bit, but then she smiled. This knowing smirk that made my blood boil.

I'd pounded on his door right after, unable to wait, but he hadn't answered, likely passed out. Axel used to never black out, no matter how much he drank, but I guess that things must have changed.

Everything's changed. Everything's gone so topsy turvy that I don't know which way is up, and it's beginning to drive me crazy. I almost forget about my ultrasound appointment, cursing when I realize that I could have asked Roland not to pick me up today.

I'd been so upset that I'd forgotten to text him that my car is working. Now I have to Uber to the appointment. I can't ask Roland to take me. That would seem strange, too intimate. I know he has a crush on me. I don't want to encourage him.

The Uber driver lifts an eyebrow when I waddle to the car and get in, breathing heavily. The baby seems to have grown tenfold in the last couple of weeks, and I'm a little ashamed that I've put off my appointment for so long.

Sure enough, the ob-gyn tsks at me about it, and also about gaining so much weight. I huff out a breath.

"I'm hungry *all the time*," I tell her. "You try carrying this thing around without sustenance."

The doctor laughs. She's a nice woman, and I know she just wants me and the baby to be healthy, but my hormones make me cranky, especially when it comes to my weight.

"It's all right, Ms. Telman. You're still within the range of healthy, I just wanted to let you know to be careful. You're right on the edge."

I grumble under my breath. I feel right on the edge, all right, on the edge of cursing her out.

The ultrasound jelly is cold, and I yelp when she dollops it on my belly with no warning.

The panic rises in my throat like it always does when there's silence on the doppler, but then the sound of the strong, fast heartbeat is like music to my ears. I sigh in relief.

The doctor frowns as she presses the wand around my belly, and my eyes widen.

"Is something wrong?"

The doctor shakes her head. "Nothing to worry about. It's just that at this point in your pregnancy, the baby should be facing downward. It seems like she might end up being breech, which just means we need to try to turn her or schedule a c-section."

I frown. "I don't want a c-section."

"You've still got four weeks left till your due date, plenty of time for her to turn. I'll print you out a pamphlet on natural ways to get her to turn, but wort case scenario, we have to do what's best for you and baby girl."

My mouth opens in shock and the doctor clamps her hand over her mouth.

"I'm sorry. That just slipped out," she laughs, and I can't believe it.

A baby girl. I was right. I'll have a little mini-me to love. I wonder if she'll have Axel's light blue eyes or my darker ones, and tears well in my eyes. I wish I could tell him. I wish I could share this with him, but it won't do any good. I wouldn't want to shackle him and have me regret this later on. He might say he wouldn't mind and be happy for a while, but how long until he started resenting me for stopping him from partying as much as he likes?

The doctor takes off her gloves. "You can get dressed now. I'll write you a note to take the afternoon off work, if you'd like," she suggests, a twinkle in her eyes.

I give her a grateful smile. "That'd be nice."

I'm already texting my supervisor that I won't be in the rest of the afternoon, and although he doesn't respond, I'm sure it'll be fine. I've barely ever taken any time off, after all.

I can't bring myself to go home and face Axel, even though it's only two in the afternoon and I could nap the rest of the day. Instead, I head to my family's house, a near mansion on the north side of town.

Six bedrooms, because my mother had wanted a big family. Unfortunately, she had infertility issues, and I was the only child they'd managed to have. As a result, I could admit that I was spoiled, at least financially.

My father was absent most of my childhood due to his job, but he's trying to make up for it now as best he can.

He's doing a good job, especially since he hasn't pressed me when I told him that I didn't know who the father was. I think my mother suspects that it might be Axel, but she hasn't said a word. I also think my father would rather think I fooled around than have this be Axel's. He never really liked him much.

Now, it's like old times again, like when I lived at home as a teenager, sneaking out to see Axel. I can't tell them that he's living next to me, and I *definitely* can't tell them that we've been hooking up again.

My mother gives me a big hug the instant I walk into the room, and I feel tears stinging my eyes again. *Damn hormones.* I cry almost every day because of them, and it's beginning to get on my nerves.

"How did it go?" she asks, since I'd texted her about my appointment, and I give her a tired smile. I didn't sleep much last night due to Axel's antics and my own anger.

"Good, I think," I tell her, handing her the pictures of the ultrasound with the baby floating around. "I found out it's a girl."

My mother squeals and hugs me again, looking intently at the pictures. "She's going to look just like you."

I laugh softly. It's not like you can tell from the blurry ultrasound pictures what the baby is going to look like, but at least I know she's healthy.

"The only problem is that she hasn't turned."

My mother nods sagely. "You were a breech baby. That's why I have this awful scar." She pokes at her belly, wrinkling her nose, and I want to roll my eyes.

She complains about that scar every moment she gets a chance, and it's one of the reasons I'm against having a c-section myself. Not the scar itself, I'd be proud to wear it, but the memories of her using hers against me.

91

"There are ways to turn her. She gave me a list."

"My mother always swore by lots of green tea, although it didn't help you turn. I'll make some."

My mother bustles around the kitchen while I slowly lower myself into a chair in the dining room, wincing at the ache in my back. Having all the extra baby weight certainly takes a toll.

"How much is she weighing in at?" my mother calls.

"Six pounds, give or take a few ounces," I tell her. I wait for a comment about my weight and how the baby only takes up six pounds, but for once, she doesn't start.

I sigh in relief, glad that she doesn't have anything to say about it. My mother can be a bit much when it comes to my body. She's always been small, petite even, and since I'm curvier and more muscular, we sometimes butt heads. She taught me her love for exercise, but I struggled with the diets she used to put me on as a teenager. She doesn't have control over what I eat and how much I exercise now, and I think sometimes it rankles her.

My mother brings in a big bowl of cut fruit, and I guess that's her way of telling me I should eat healthier. I pop a couple of grapes in my mouth, grateful for the food since I skipped lunch to go to my appointment.

"So, what was going on the other night when you called me?" My mother's voice seems nonchalant, but I know that she truly wants to know.

I shrug. "Just hormones, I guess."

My mother looks up at me over her small reading glasses. I guess she must have been reading the newspaper before I arrived, because she doesn't wear them as often as she should.

"Harley," she says, and I know that she doesn't believe me.

I sigh. "We should wait for Dad to talk about this."

My mother arches a well-groomed eyebrow. "It must be serious."

I give her a wan smile. "Not *so* serious," I mumble, popping more fruit into my mouth to keep from having to talk.

* * *

I take a nap on the couch before my father arrives, just in time for dinner. I wake up feeling refreshed, but still dreading this conversation. My parents were there to witness my struggles with Axel's constant absences, and I know they will worry that he's living so close to me.

My mother clears her throat after she sits down, everyone having their perfectly portioned plates of meat and vegetables.

"Was there something you wanted to tell us, Harley?"

I nearly choke on my water. I'm not ready to start talking about this, but I guess I have no choice.

"Uh, you know that duplex that I moved into?"

My mother nods and my father is scrolling through emails on his phone, barely paying attention, which isn't unusual.

I take in a deep breath. "Well, someone moved into the other side. Someone... that I know."

"Oh! Well, that sounds nice!" My mother chirps. "You need to have more people around. You've been so *isolated* since you got pregnant, dear, it's not good for you."

My father looks up from his phone. "Who is it? Anyone we know?"

I swallow hard. "Uh, yeah. I think you know him pretty well. It's Axel."

I blurt it out, not wanting to hesitate.

My father's face changes instantly, his mouth turning down at the corners, and my mother sighs and rubs a hand across her face.

"Oh, goodness," she mutters.

"Your ex-husband moved in next door to you, and you haven't *told* us?" My father's voice booms across the long table, and I wince.

"I *am* telling you. I'm trying to move out, but there are no properties available that have a room I can use for a nursery," I try to explain in a meek voice, but my father isn't having it.

"Why should *you* be the one to move? What's his angle, anyway? Is he trying to get back into your life? Weasel his way in?"

"N-nothing like that, Dad," I stutter, finding it hard to lie to him.

"You don't need this kind of stress, honey." My mother's voice is a lot softer than my father's, and I relax a little.

I sigh. "I know. It's been... difficult."

"Well, you'll just have to move back in here," my father announces, as if it's a done deal. "We have plenty of extra space, after all, and you and the baby will be welcome."

"She found out it's a girl, honey!" My mother tells him, clearly trying to change the subject, but I frown.

My father chuckles. "Another baby girl. I'll be surrounded."

"Wait just a minute. Back up. I'm not moving back in here. I need my own space to take care of the baby—" I begin, and my father holds up a hand to stop me, a common gesture in our household.

"I won't hear of it, Harley. Axel will just keep trying to get

94

back together with you, and you know that you're not right for each other. He's always treated you like an afterthought to his damn music, and you deserve better than that."

My frown grows deeper. I can't deny that I'd thought much the same thing several times during our marriage, but there's some part of me that hates it coming out of my father's mouth.

"I don't think that matters now, Dad. He needs a place to stay, and I can't just kick him out."

"I don't see why not. Don't you pay the rent there?" My father pauses. "In fact, why don't I just buy the whole duplex? Then you won't have to worry about him living there."

I gape at him. "Dad, you can't do that. You can't just buy it out from under me. I'm renting to own so that it can be *my* place."

"It'll still be your place," Dad says dismissively. "Of course, I'll give it to you. I'll even put it in your name."

"How generous of you," I say dryly, and my mother gives me a sharp look.

"Don't sass, Harley," she warns, and I feel sixteen all over again.

I hate this. I hate feeling like a kid all over again, and that's exactly how it will be if I move back in.

I stand up with some effort, pushing my chair back. "I think I need to go home now."

"You're not going back there," my father insists.

"Honey," my mother put a hand on his, trying to stop the fight, but it's too late.

"You don't get to tell me what to do anymore, Dad. I'm twenty-six years old. I'm not a little girl anymore." I'm not shouting, but it's a near thing. "That's why I can't move back in here. I need my own space, my own time to learn to be a mother."

"But, Harley, we could *help* you," my mother says, her bottom lip trembling.

Great. Here come the water works. My mother's biggest manipulation tool is crying, but I'm not going to let it work this time.

"We'll talk about this later," I manage, grabbing my purse. I wait for a moment for my father to stand up and continue arguing, but he doesn't, huffing out a breath and looking down at his phone again.

When I make it outside and call Uber, I'm almost crying again.

This time, I *can't* blame it on the hormones.

Chapter 15

Axel

I don't start drinking until Harley doesn't come home after nine in the evening. I've only managed a few slugs of tequila when she pulls into the drive, and I'm grateful that I'm only tipsy instead of drunk.

If I was drunk, I probably would have been a lot meaner about what I have to ask her.

She looks at me, bags under her eyes, and part of me thinks that I shouldn't ask, that it isn't the right time. But when is the right time to ask the love of your life this question?

"Who's the father?" I blurt out, and it sounds like a demand.

Harley sighs. "I'm not talking about this."

I stand up, no stumble in sight thanks to the high tolerance I've built since Harley and I split.

"Harley, please," I beg. "I need to know."

Harley looks up at me, her blue eyes still seeming tired and red, like she's been crying.

"Why does it matter? What are you going to do? Track him down? Beat him up?"

I blink at her. I can't deny that those two options have occurred to me more than once, but really, I just feel like I *need* to know, like it'll drive me crazy if I don't.

"N-no," I stutter. "Nothing like that. I just... I'm curious." I take a couple steps toward her and she backs up, resting her back against the brick of her duplex.

"It's nobody," Harley dismisses, and I huff out a breath, frustration rising in me. "No one that you know. Don't worry about it."

"Don't *worry* about it? Harley, it drives me crazy every goddamn day and you're telling me not to worry about it?"

"It doesn't *matter*, Axel!" she bursts out, and I can't help it. I slam my hand above her, the brick stinging my palms.

"Of course it does, Harley," I hiss. "You let someone else touch you. You let someone else inside what's mine. It fucking *matters.*"

Harley's breathing hard as she looks up at me and I wonder if she'll hit me, push me away like she used to when we fought and I got in her face, but instead she snakes her arms around my neck.

She stands up on her tiptoes, traces just the tip of her tongue along my collarbone, making my skin tingle and heat flood to my belly.

"You've got me, now, so it doesn't matter," she murmurs, and I moan when she sucks a mark at the base of my throat.

I want to say again that it fucking *does* matter, that I need to know who she spread her legs for, but I'm weakening. Goddamnit, the things she does to me. I can't resist her. I never could.

"Harley," I murmur, and I tilt her chin up and kiss her, hard and hungry, our teeth gnashing together in my hurry. "We can't keep doing this."

"We can't? Why not?" She pouts a little, her eyes half-lidded, and I let out a long breath.

"Because I want more," I tell her, not knowing that I'm going to say it until I do. I'm just as surprised as she is. I was sure that I was going to give in.

Harley sighs. "I know," she says, and her voice shakes.

I trace my thumb along her cheekbone slowly. "Why won't you let me in, sweetheart? Let me help you."

Let me love you, I want to say but don't. It feels like too much, like my heart is already close to breaking all over again.

Harley's blue eyes well with tears as she looks up at me.

"I can't," she whispers, and slips her arms from my neck, ducking under my arm to go inside to her duplex.

I stare at the brick where she'd been standing, wondering how badly I'll fuck up my knuckles if I punch there the way I want to, but I decide against it.

At least I still have half a bottle of tequila.

I have another headache when I wake up the next morning, and it's no wonder, since I'd finished the bottle while looking at our wedding album, flipping through the pictures that contained all the memories I wish that I could forget.

I don't know what to do. I don't know where to go from here. Do I give up? The very thought feels like a rock in my stomach. My heart aches every time I think about her, but I can't imagine not being around her, not seeing her every day.

The time we spent apart has already been like hell to me, and I can't imagine willingly going back to that. But alternately, could I be around her like this and not have her?

I could have her physically, that part helps, but it's not enough. I want all of her, not just her body. I don't know if just having this piece of her will be enough or if it will kill me wanting more.

I take a shower, thinking of what to do next. The only thing I can do is try to keep talking to her, keep the communication open. I had ordered a part for her sink that I needed to install, and that could be a way to get back in, to somehow get closer.

After showering and dressing, I take my toolbox to her door and I don't have to knock, she's bustling out dressed in her work clothes. She stares at me.

"What are you doing?"

I shrug. "I got the part for your sink, thought I could fix it while you were at work."

Harley lets out a long breath. "Do you promise not to snoop?"

I raise an eyebrow, smiling slightly. "Will I find anything good?"

Harley shakes her head and I think I see the beginnings of a smile at the corners of her lips. It's not enough, but it's something.

"Lock up when you're finished," she says, and I hold back a whoop of victory. It seems small, her letting me fix her sink, but I know Harley, and she's fiercely independent. She doesn't ask for help, and if you push it on her, she usually won't take it.

It's a step in the right direction, and I hum a little while fixing the sink, my mood lifting. She also took the Beetle to work instead of that asshole picking her up, so that makes my mood better, too.

When I'm done, my shirt is covered in dirty water but I stand in the kitchen for a long moment, looking over the island into the living room. There's a crib, not even half put together, piled in the corner.

I bite my bottom lip, thinking. It's not like I approve of Harley being pregnant, in fact, it drives me crazy not knowing who put that baby inside her. But if I want Harley back, don't I have to accept it? I have to accept that she's going to have a baby, going to keep some kid with some other guy's eyes. I let out a long breath.

That's going to be a lot harder than any of the rest of it. I walk over toward the crib and start reading the instructions.

By the time Harley returns, I'm only halfway through it. Damn those Swedish instructions. She gapes at me from the doorway.

"Axel?"

I twist around to look at her, a small wrench in my hand. I smile at her.

"How was work?"

"Axel, you don't have to put together the crib. I just need the sink fixed—" she begins, but I stand up, holding up my hands to stop her.

"Just got on a roll and started it, that's all. I'm sorry."

Harley looks at me, her blue eyes confused but not angry.

"You don't have to be sorry," she says softly, and I wonder if she's going to kiss me again. To keep her from doing so, I clear my throat and pick up my toolbox.

"I'll get out of your hair."

She stares at me for a moment longer, then looks away.

I can't stop smiling as I head across the garage to my duplex. She's letting me in, one small moment at a time.

Chapter 16

Harley

Walking in on Axel working on the crib threw me through a loop and I plop down on the couch after he leaves, my head spinning. I know (and have known ever since we split) that Axel wants to get back together, but I never thought that he would accept the baby, as well.

That's one thing that's been holding me back: if Axel can't accept that I'm going to have a baby, we'll never be right for each other. The fact that it's *his* baby shouldn't matter. Him not knowing it's his is a way to make sure he isn't staying for the wrong reasons. If he decides he wants to stay anyway, I'll know it was his choice, not an obligation he felt toward me or the baby.

I *know* that he loves me, deep down, I just don't know if he loves me enough to put me first sometimes. I can admit that I'm a little jealous and that I can be paranoid. But I witnessed enough growing up that I want to make sure I'm not an afterthought. That *my daughter* isn't an afterthought.

When we first started, I'd go with him to his gigs and we'd always be together, but then I started college and my partying times had to end because I had to focus on school. He would go By the time he joined the band, it was all about the fans and how he had to give them some attention because they had to build a fan base. So, he was out all night partying and I felt invisible. Undesired. I knew he was faithful and loved me, but I also knew how fans were and the lengths they would go to just to be with any of the guys. So, after years of asking him to choose me, to please stay home or come home early and never once getting my way, could I trust him now? After just this week I'd walked in on some girl kissing him in our garage?

I groan and roll over onto my side on the couch, staring over at the crib, which is now almost halfway put together. If Axel can accept me *and* the baby, that might mean things could be different.

Am I actually considering giving him another chance? I avert my eyes from the crib. I'm really uncomfortable, watching the ceiling fan go around and around. I'm exhausted from work, the baby having been moving around all of last night after my fight with my parents. I drape my forearm over my eyes, closing them and hoping that I can catch a nap.

I wake up with a start. Someone is yelling outside, and I try to scramble up off the couch. It's a struggle, and as I finally rise, I waddle to the door. It takes me a few minutes to get out to the garage.

"I'm not leaving," Axel says just as I walk outside, and to my dismay, I see my father standing in my driveway, glaring at my ex-husband.

"I don't think I was asking," my father shot back. "I'm in the process of purchasing this duplex, and we don't want any tenants."

"I think you should look into the rules for tenants," Axel

drawls, seeming calm while my father's voice keeps raising. "You have to have a reason to kick someone out."

"I have plenty of reasons!" my father yells, and I huff out a breath and walk up to him.

"What are you doing?" I hiss, and my father barely looks at me, still staring down Axel as if they're in the midst of a Western duel.

"He was a shitty husband and he's a shitty tenant," my father insists. "He has to go."

"You can't just kick him out, Dad, that's not how it works."

"I've got this house in escrow, so it's only a matter of time." My father takes a menacing step toward Axel. "In the meantime, you leave my baby girl alone. She's moved on. She divorced you."

Axel doesn't answer, his jaw clenched tight like he's gritting his teeth.

I push at my Dad's shoulder until he reluctantly starts to walk back to his car.

"I don't need your help, Dad. I'm going to figure this out. Tell them you're not going to buy the duplex," I order, and my father shakes his head.

"It's a done deal, petal." He hasn't used that pet name for me in years, and I resent that he's using it now, to butter me up.

"I didn't ask you to do that!" I burst out, but my yelling doesn't seem to faze my father.

"Tell him he has thirty days after the close of escrow in a week," my father snarls, and gets back into his car, pulling out of the drive while I stand there, flabbergasted.

I turn to look at Axel, and his brows are furrowed together, blue eyes flashing with anger.

"Did you do this?" he demands, and I blink at him.

"What? Of *course* I didn't!" I can't believe that he'd even think that of me.

"It seems real convenient, Harley. You wanted me gone, so you went to Daddy to ask him to buy the house," Axel accuses.

"I wouldn't do that, Axel. You *know* me." I insist, tears springing to the backs of my eyes. I want him to believe me. I *need* him to believe me.

"Do I?" Axel asks, his voice softer but no less harsh. "I don't know that I do, Harley. You let me in, spread your legs for me, but you have someone else's baby growing in your belly, and now suddenly, you want me out? Is it because I stopped putting out? Is that all you want from me?"

I stare at him, heartbreak and anger warring up inside me when it had just been sadness before.

"Fuck you," I manage, my voice shaking. "You're right; you don't know me at all."

I storm back into my house and slam the door behind me, locking the top lock. I'm sure he won't be here tomorrow morning to fix my sink or put together the crib.

I hear his motorcycle revving up and I look out the window to see him peeling out onto the driveway. I check my phone to see that earlier today he'd sent me a text, an invitation to a concert here in Tucson.

"Fuck," I mutter, looking down at my phone with tears blurring my vision. I might have gone if we hadn't gotten into this fight. It'd been so long since I'd seen him play.

My sniffles turn to sobs, and I head into the bedroom, sitting down and scrolling through my contacts. I need someone to talk to but it's not like I can call my mother or father. Finally, my thumb hovers over an old contact. My childhood best friend: Charlotte. I'd cut her out after she'd bought me the pregnancy test. I hadn't answered any of her calls in months.

I draw in a deep, shaky breath and hit the call button.

"Hello?" she answers, and the sound of her voice makes me let out a sob.

"Charlotte? It's me, Harley," I choke out, sniffling, and there's a long pause on the other end of the line.

"Oh my God, Harley. Are you okay? Shit, are you crying?"

"I'm okay," I tell her but then choke out another sob, unable to help myself. "I just... I need someone to talk to," I admit, and Charlotte is quiet again, so quiet I wonder for a moment if she had hung up.

"Where are you?"

I give her my address and we hang up after I can't stop crying enough to make my words make sense. I lie down on my bed until she gets there and I waddle to the door, my sobs finally having turned to sniffles.

Charlotte's eyes nearly bulge out of her head when she sees me. "Holy *shit!*"

I tug her inside and she hugs me tightly. "Jesus, Harley, I didn't know the test was positive. I thought all this time you'd run off to a new city and become a big-time journalist or something."

I snort. "Yeah, right." I pause, feeling miserable. A sob racks me.

"What happened? Something with your parents?"

"So much has happened," I tell her, sitting down on the couch and rubbing my belly to get baby girl out of my ribs.

I explain everything to her, starting with Axel moving in and ending with my father showing up and making a scene, and the way Axel and I had fought.

Charlotte listens, offering me tissues from her purse, and nodding here and there.

"So much has happened, Harley. You have to be *beyond* stressed out. It's not good for the baby."

I rub a hand across my face. "I know. I've kind of been ignoring everything, but Axel, you know how that goes."

"I do," she says dryly. She'd been there when Axel and I split. "So, the baby...it's Axel's?"

I nod miserably, but it feels like something heavy has been lifted off my shoulders to finally tell someone. "I haven't told him. I don't want him to know. Actually, other than me, you're the only one who knows the truth."

Charlotte stares at me. "What? Why?"

"Because he'll never give up, Charlie. You know Axel." We'd all known each other since we were teenagers, having all attended the high school at the same time.

"Looks to me like he hasn't given up even without knowing the truth about the baby."

I pause. "I guess you're right. He's just so *angry* with me, Charlotte, you don't understand. It's like he doesn't trust me anymore."

Charlotte raises a black eyebrow. "Doesn't that sound familiar?"

I give her a look. "Don't start."

"I'm serious, Harl. Axel has said the very same thing to you, about how you didn't trust him. You are now feeling in the flesh what he felt for all those years."

"That's not fair," I argue, and she shrugs.

"All's fair in love and war, they say," she jokes, and I manage to give her a wan smile.

"I just...I thought that things were different, but now that I think about it, I don't think things are that different after all. After all, he brought that girl home—"

"Axel's single now, Harley. You can't be mad at him for seeing other people."

"The hell I can't," I say firmly, and Charlotte laughs.

"You two, always so possessive, even when we were kids. Besides, how can you blame him? He thinks you are pregnant with someone else's baby! It's time to grow up, for both of you."

I take in a deep breath, having forgotten how level-headed she could be. And she is right.

"I missed you," I say, leaning my head against her shoulder, and she puts an arm around me.

"I missed you, too," she says softly. "I missed giving you advice that I knew you would never take."

I bark out a surprised laugh. "I take *some* of your advice."

"Like what?" she asks, and I have to think for a long, long moment.

"Well, I took the pregnancy test, didn't I?"

Charlotte shakes her head, laughing. "I guess so."

"So, what do I do, Charlie? Where do I go from here?"

Charlie looks over at the half-finished crib in the corner. "I think right now, you have to do what's best for the baby. You have to relieve yourself of some of this stress."

I sigh heavily. "How the hell do I do that?"

"Maybe you could come and stay with me and Daniel?" Charlotte offers, something hopeful in her voice.

"Wait, Daniel? Daniel Jacobs?" I ask, and Charlotte sticks out her left hand, showing me a big ring on her finger.

She grins. "Yeah, I'm Charlotte Jacobs, now."

Unlike me and Axel who were glued at the hip until I went to college and couldn't keep up anymore, she and Daniel had been on and off again since high school, and mostly off in the last few years, so I'm surprised.

I hug her tightly. "I'm so happy for you!"

"Then do me a favor. Come and stay with me for a few days," Charlotte insistes.

I bite my bottom lip. "I don't want to intrude on a couple of newlyweds."

Charlotte waves her hand dismissively. "We've been together forever, we're not exactly newlyweds, even if we just got married three months ago. Besides, you know Daniel. He's not the most romantic guy."

Axel has always been the opposite, but I don't want to think about that right now.

I take Charlotte's hand. "I'd love to have a sleepover with you."

Charlotte grins, and I know I've made the right decision.

"After work tomorrow," I promise. "I'll stay a few days."

Chapter 17

Axel

I can't drink as much tequila as I want to, since we're performing tonight, and I'm early for rehearsal. Locke and Jackson are at the bar and they beckon me over for a beer. When I chug it, Locke gives me a look.

"Don't ask," Jackson warns, and Locke shrugs, sipping his beer.

Samuel comes in a little late but he comes ready to play, wearing a pair of ripped jeans and a Pink Floyd t-shirt.

I miss two of my queues in rehearsal and Locke and Jackson both groan.

"Sorry, sorry," I mumble. I know that I haven't been practicing enough, too focused on Harley and everything that's been going on.

The next run-through, I get everything right on point, and Jackson sighs in relief. I think he thought I was going to fuck up our whole concert, but I had no plans to ruin the one good thing in my life.

Being a part of Jack and the Spades makes me feel at home in a way that I haven't since I moved in next door to

Accidental Secret Daddy

Harley, and I'm grateful for the distraction, especially after our fight.

I can't stop thinking about it, how she'd run to her father, who she knew hated me, and gotten him to buy the place out from under me. I'm not about to go without a fight, regardless of her father's money.

The man had once offered me ten grand to leave town like we were in some eighties rom-com, and I'd of course, said no. I'd never even told Harley about it. I don't want Harley to see her father as some kind of villain, even though at times he'd acted like one.

"No more tequila, okay?" Jackson warns, clapping a hand on my shoulder to show that he doesn't mean it harshly.

I nod. No more tequila, at least, not until the concert is over. Beer will keep my head light throughout our sets. Out in the crowd, there are a dozen blonde girls, but none of them are Harley.

I don't know why I expected that she might show up anyway, after everything that happened tonight. It makes me feel depressed but the opening bars of "Amped Up," the song I'd penned right after my split with Harley, make me feel a bit better. The beat opens me up somehow, makes me feel lighter than I have in weeks, maybe months.

The first half of the concert goes by without a hitch, and other than some technical difficulties with the amps (which is a little ironic since it happened just after we performed "Amped Up"), the second half goes by well. The guys whoop and holler along with the crowd after my last solo, which I have to admit I killed.

Everyone's in a good mood and the liquor is flowing for all except Locke and Gemma, but they are as cheerful as the rest of us anyway.

111

"Tonight was a success!" Gemma announces, clinking her shot glass with me. "And part of it is thanks to you, Axel. You brought in a big crowd from social media. We made *bank* in covers and merch tonight!"

Locke grumbles a little at Gemma giving me praise, but despite the concert putting me in a good mood, I'm not quite feeling well enough to flirt back with her to rile him up. That's unusual, but I guess with everything going on with Harley, it's not surprising.

Samuel is the one who whoops at the amount of money we made, and I chuckle, knowing he must be a bit tipsy from the beer we'd had during the set. He's not a drinker like the rest of us are, and it's pretty funny when he gets lit. The fact that I can laugh means that I'm in a better mood than earlier, and I try my best to enjoy myself.

I ignore the girls that try to get my attention, though, knowing that no matter how drunk I get, their touch won't feel like Harley's. It'll feel wrong, somehow, broken, and I don't want to feel like that tonight. I just want to forget that women exist, minus Gemma, of course, who's become one of my best friends.

Locke's attached to her at the hip, though, and I smile fondly at them dirty dancing in the middle of the club. Their back and forth on tour had kept my mind off Harley, even if I'd gotten a sock in the nose for my trouble.

Everything seems to be lining up for a great night, even though I'm probably too drunk by the time they do last call at the club around three in the morning. It's after daylight when we arrive home, and I have no idea what time it actually is, since I'd left my phone at home, knowing that I have a tendency to drunk dial my ex-wife when I drink.

"Everything's gonna be okay, Axel, you know that, right?" Gemma says, and I raise an eyebrow. Somehow I'd missed that Locke is our designated driver. Gemma turns around, looking at me seriously.

"We love you. And you deserve to have what we have," she tells me.

"You do," Locke states, more softly, looking at me in the rearview mirror. "Why don't you talk to Harley?"

"Now?" I ask incredulously, looking down at my shirt, which I'd spilled nearly a whole margarita on.

Gemma laughs. "Not *now*, you idiot, but sometime soon. After you sleep it off."

We pull up in the garage just as Harley is leaving, and she frowns when I stumble out of the backseat of the car, bracing myself on the driver's side of the Beetle.

"Sorry," I mumble, and start to walk, albeit unsteadily, over to my duplex.

"Axel," Harley calls. "Are you okay to get home?"

"It's just... right there," I insist, pointing somewhere in the direction of my duplex.

Harley sighs. "You're trashed. Look, I don't think you can unlock the door in this state, why don't you stay at my place?"

I give her a huge grin, and she glares at me. "On the couch," she says firmly, and I pout a little but let her put her arm around my waist and lead me into her duplex.

I plop down on the couch, honestly mostly because I'm barely able to stand, and Harley wrinkles her nose.

"Shower," she demands, and then looking at the way I'm swaying on the couch, she amends, "Bath."

"You gonna bathe me?" I ask, not even knowing if I'm coherent. It seems like the last three shots have hit me all at once, and everything is going in and out of focus.

"I have work," she says, but she's still biting her lip.

"Call in," I plead. "Need you, Harley."

Harley lets out a low curse and brings out her phone, texting something.

It seems like there are two of Harleys while she runs the water, and I manage to undress myself. She helps me into the tub with a grunt.

I stare after her as the water continues to run, feeling warm and lovely against my alcohol-flushed skin.

"Wash my back?" I ask, my voice hoarse from the liquor, and Harley bites down on her bottom lip, a familiar habit. I know she's thinking about it, at least, and I hide a grin.

She runs a washcloth down my back and I groan, her touch feeling amazing even through the booze haze.

"Are you still mad at me?" I ask softly, trying to focus on her face. I'm not mad anymore. I know that Harley wouldn't have gone to her father, but earlier, I couldn't help thinking that she wanted to be rid of me, that it would be easier for her if I was gone.

Harley sighs. "I don't know, Axel. I don't know much of anything anymore."

I frown, not liking the way her voice sounds, how *down* she seems.

"What does that mean?" I try hard not to slur my words and my head clears just a little.

Harley's crying, tears streaming down her cheeks. I make a distressed sound in the back of my throat and cup her face in my hands, thumbing away tears.

"It means I don't know what to do, Axel. I don't know where to go from here."

"Me either," I admit. That's what I'd been thinking earlier tonight, actually. It's like we're on the same page, even if it's a confusing one. I think of what Gemma had said, that I should sleep it off first, and shut my mouth, not wanting to say too much.

"Axel?" Harley tilts her head, looking at me curiously. "What's wrong?"

I'm tired all of a sudden, exhausted, and I don't know how to keep what I want to say locked away anymore.

"Everything," I say hoarsely. "Everything's wrong without you, Harley. Why did you leave me? Why did you send me away? I never knew... But whatever it was I did, I'm sorry. I'm so, so sorry."

Harley's biting her lip again, but I'm too drunk and tired to know what it means.

Softly whispering the words, she says, "Because I felt I was just another piece of furniture. Like I didn't matter anymore."

"How could you think that? You are and always were the most important thing in my life." How can she not know this? How could she ever doubt my love? Where had I gone so wrong?

"Was I? Because no matter how many times I hinted, asked or full out begged, you never once chose to come home to me after a show. You always, always chose the fans, the parties. And I figured I didn't matter anymore." Her eyes fall to the floor and her tears keep cascading down her face.

"Harley..." Her name comes out so broken. I can't begin to think how she even felt, because that was never my intent. We were building a fan base and interaction with our fans is key. I thought she understood that it was something I had to do. We all had. Had I known this was how she felt, I'd have figured some alternatives, some way to balance things better, talk to the guys and see some other way I could help. It was never my intention to have to choose between her and the band, but didn't she know she'd always come first? She was my forever!

"What if..." she begins and then clears her throat and starts again, her voice shaking. "What if for today, we just pretend?"

I'm too raw to speak right now, so I just nod slowly. I'm not sure what she means by that but I don't care, as long as I get to be with her for a little while longer, wake up with her in my arms in a few hours, because I do have to crash soon, even if all I want is to soak every second I have with her. Even if all I want is to show her how much she matters to me. How much I care. How sorry I am, for everything.

"Pretend everything's okay?" I ask, finding my voice as Harley tilts my head back, pouring water over my head with a cup to wash my hair.

Harley nods. "Pretend everything's okay, like there's no more obstacles. Forget about the past and the future. Just enjoy today as if nothing had ever gone wrong."

I sigh in relief, tears welling in my eyes. "That sounds wonderful."

This is what I want, what I've always wanted. I just want her to let me in, to give me one day, one night, and maybe then I can get past it. I say that, but she's given me these nights before and it doesn't change how much I love her.

I'll fight for her for as long as she lets me. I'll take what I can get, until she stops giving it to me. Maybe that makes me pathetic. Maybe that makes me a sap, but I can't help it. I love her so much that I don't know what to do with it. It sits on my chest, spreads through my veins, and it's like I can't breathe with how much I want her.

The bath sobers me up a bit and I'm able to sling a towel around me and follow Harley to her bedroom. I slide up behind her, pressing my body against hers, even though there's no way I'm sober enough to make love to her. I want to be as close as I can, want to feel her skin through the nightie she's changed into.

"I love you, Harley," I say, not expecting her to say it back, and for a long moment, she's silent.

"I love you too, Axel." Her voice is so quiet it's almost a whisper, but it's enough. I sigh happily and bury my face in her sweet-smelling hair, passing out easily.

Chapter 18

Harley

I wake up slowly, blinking, with Axel's arms tight around me. He's scooped one hand underneath my waist and locked his hands together with his other arm above my waist, his face buried in my neck.

Yesterday and last night had been great. He had slept part of the day, then we'd talked about sweet nothings, ate, and made love until we fell asleep in each other's arms again. Now our bubble in time had come to an end and I had to deal with the consequences.

The first consequence seems to be that Axel won't let me up. No matter how much I wiggle, his arms stay locked around me, and then a low moan rumbles from his chest. I can feel him growing hard against my ass and I bite down on my lip to keep from pushing back against him.

It's ridiculous, how much I still want him. I know I shouldn't after he'd stayed out partying with the band again before he came home.

Home. That's what this feels like, in the end. Axel's arms around me feel like coming home, and I have to get out of here.

"Axel, let me up," I say. I'd called into work on a Friday, and that wasn't going to go over well with my supervisor. Maybe if I offer to come in for a few hours today and make up for it...

"Why? It's Saturday," Axel murmurs against my neck, leaving open mouthed kisses there and on my shoulder that make my skin tingle and pop out with goosebumps.

"I might need to go into work," I protest, but it's weak. *I'm* weak, with his arms around me and his erection pressing up against me. I still want him. God, will I always want him?

"Not yet," Axel pleads, biting down on my shoulder and pulling up my nightie, his hands roving over my thighs and ass. "Just give me a few minutes. I could slide right inside, I bet. You're already worked up, I can tell."

I let out a moan and twist my head to kiss him, hoping to distract him enough to wiggle out of his arms. Axel's smarter than that, though, because he locks his forearms around my waist, just above the swell of my belly and ruts against me again.

I lift my left leg and he grunts and shifts to slide inside me, groaning low in his chest, almost like a growl.

I give in, closing my eyes, letting myself be weak, letting my body love the way he's stretching me out as he moves his hips slow and steady.

"God, I miss this. I miss this every day, Harley."

"You miss my pussy?" I breathe, and Axel groans louder.

"Yes," he admits, "but I miss so much more."

He doesn't elaborate, and I'm glad. He was so soft and sweet yesterday that I could barely stand it. I can't stay mad at him for anything, it turns out.

"I miss this, too," I confess, and Axel takes my chin in his hand and kisses me again, slow and dirty.

I suck on his tongue, knowing exactly what he likes, and his hips buck, hitting a sweet spot that makes me moan into his mouth.

It's only a few more thrusts before I begin to come, gasping out his name, and when he spills inside me it takes me a moment to realize what he's saying.

"I love you, Harley. Love you so fucking much," he's panting, and it feels like an arrow through my heart.

Because I know it's true. I know that he loves me, but I also know that we're not right for each other and it feels like my heart might split wide open. I have to protect myself, yes, but most of all, I have to protect the little girl that I carry inside me. The little piece of him that will forever be mine.

"You have to go," I tell him, my voice shaking, and Axel stiffens.

"Don't make me go," he pleads, kissing along my back and down my spine, but I pull away from him. He slips out of me and I stand up, pulling down my nightie.

"I can't do this, Axel," I sniffle. "I can't do this again."

"Why *not?* Harley, please, just... talk to me. I'll change, I promise. I'll do anything you want me to. Just let me in. Why can't we try again?" He sits up in my bed, looking at me so earnestly that it just makes me cry harder.

"The baby," I begin, but then dissolve into sobs.

Axel crawls across the bed, trying to grab me around the waist and pull me back down, but I step away, wiping angrily at my eyes.

"What about the baby? Have you... have you been talking to the father again?" Axel asks slowly, something like realization dawning on his handsome face.

"Well, yes, but—" I'm this close to telling him. I'm this close to letting everything out, getting it off my chest and letting the chips fall where they may.

Axel's face sours instantly. "Who is he? It's that asshole who keeps coming to pick you up, isn't it? Someone from work? Someone Daddy approves of?" he spits out, and I take in a deep, shaking breath, trying to stop crying.

"You don't know what you're talking about, Axel, please, just listen to me—"

But he's past listening, and I can see it all over his face. He stands up, stalking around to find his shirt and jeans, pulling them on while I'm still crying and trying to get words out.

"You don't understand, Axel, the baby is—"

"I don't want to talk about this anymore." Axel says stonily. "I don't want to talk about the baby or the father or whatever other excuse you have, Harley. I was willing to try. I was willing to accept that you fucked someone else while I was still reeling, that you got *pregnant* and didn't even breathe a word to me, but I can't deal with this anymore. I can't do this back and forth. Either you want me, or you don't. And every single step of the way you keep showing me that you don't. I've just been too blind to see it."

"Axel," I gasp, unable to keep the tears from spilling out of my eyes, and he looks at me for a long moment, as if he wants to come to me and God, I want him to. I want him to take me in his arms and tell me everything is going to be okay.

Instead, he turns on his heel and leaves my duplex. A few moments later, the sound of his motorcycle revving up comes through my open kitchen window, and I collapse on the couch, sobbing.

Finally, after I feel like all the water in my body has

come out of my eyes, I stop crying and manage to call Charlotte.

"Charlie? I could really use that sleepover now," I ask with a blocked nose.

* * *

Charlotte comes to get me and, on the way, I can barely tell her anything because I keep wanting to cry again. Another crying spell and I don't think that I can stop, and Charlotte doesn't push, thank God.

When we arrive at her place, Daniel, her husband, is sitting in the living room, watching some football game. Charlotte gives him a look and he makes himself scarce. She flips the television to some horror channel, remembering that I said absolutely no romantic comedies.

"Thank you for this, Charlotte. I couldn't stay in that duplex one more second," I tell her, squeezing her hand gratefully.

"Did something happen?" she asks, and I groan.

"Nothing more than me being an *idiot*," I mutter. "I let him in again."

Charlotte raises an eyebrow. "By let him in, you mean...."

I nod, knowing what she's asking. "Yes, I slept with him." I sigh heavily. "I know it's stupid but he was drunk and he was being so sweet..."

Charlotte chuckles softly. "Axel's always been a sweet drunk. I remember that one fight that you guys had over that friend of yours—"

My eyes widen as I remember. "Jason! He was just a guy that I went to school with, but Axel couldn't *stand* him."

"Exactly! And you told him he didn't trust you and you guys had that big drag out fight and he got *shitfaced* before the graduation party and went to your house to try and serenade you."

I laugh out loud. "He ended up at my father's window. I thought Dad was going to kill him."

"He showed up at that graduation party with a bloody nose and a promise ring." Charlotte reminds me.

I take in a deep breath through my nostrils and let it out slowly, the baby kicking my ribs uncomfortably, as if she knows we are talking about her daddy.

"Sweet isn't always enough, Charlie."

"What *would* be enough?" I stare at her for a moment, and she props her elbow on the couch to cup her chin.

I think for a long moment. "I don't ask for much, Charlie, really. I just want him to choose me. I want him to show me that I matter too."

"You want him to stop performing? Give up his music? His dream?" Charlotte asks, and I shake my head vehemently.

"God, no! I'd never ask him to do that. I just... I want him to make me feel like I'm a priority too." I rub my belly. "I can't be with him and have his baby knowing that we'll be last on the list behind Jack and the Spades and the fans and the partying and whatever else."

Charlotte hums in the back of her throat. "Have you ever asked him what his priorities are? Do you think that he would say the Spades?"

I blink. I'd never thought about that. But it doesn't matter, and I said as much to Charlotte.

"Even if he said it was me, actions speak louder than words."

Charlotte pinches the bridge of her nose between her

index and middle finger, as if frustrated. "He had a concert last night, right? But he ended up in your bed instead of some groupie's."

I frown, but she has a point.

"He could have any number of girls at that concert, Harls, but he came home to you. Doesn't that mean something to you?"

Fuck. I hate it when my best friend is right. I had barely seen Axel work on any of his music, had only heard him practicing once or twice. He'd been focused on me, and in the end, isn't that what I want? I want to be number one, and he's been making me his number one priority ever since he moved in to the duplex.

"What if it's just because we're split up, though?" I ask hesitantly. "What if it all ends the second I say that we'll try again?"

Charlotte shrugs. "What if Daniel in there cheats on me? Finds some floozy at work and leaves me for a younger woman? Anything can happen, Harley. We can all get hurt, but we take the risk because it's worth the potential for pain, right?"

I gnaw on my bottom lip, a bad habit I need to break myself of.

"I can't imagine losing him again, Charlie. I don't think I'd make it."

"You're losing him *now*, Harley," Charlotte says gently, and my heart aches because she's right.

She's right and I don't have a single clue what to do about it.

Chapter 19

Axel

After Harley kicks me out (*again*), I do the only thing that ever makes me feel better in situations when I feel down: I write music. This song won't have the high-energy party music sound that "Amped Up" does. Hell, it might even be more of a ballad, which Jack and the Spades is known for.

Our ballads are famous among our fans, but Jackson and Locke write those. Samuel and I are the ones that write the hard rock songs, the ones that people jump up and down and dance to. Today, however, I can't bring myself to write a hard rock song when my heart feels so heavy.

I'm playing with the melody when my phone buzzes in my pocket.

I don't recognize the number, but I answer it anyway with a tired, "Hello?"

"Axel!" Sophie's voice chirps in my ear, triggering my hangover and making my head hurt.

I wince and move the phone a bit away from my ear.

"Sophie," I greet her. "What's up?"

"I was thinking it's been a few days since we posted

anything, and I have some video footage from the concert last night – I couldn't catch you after it was over, but I wanted to talk to you."

She's almost babbling and I remember what Harley had said, that she'd kissed me. I figure Harley is exaggerating, maybe Sophie was helping my drunk ass inside. That seems more likely than her wanting to kiss my tequila breath.

I know I'm handsome, but God knows I've been a mess the past several months. Harley has the tendency to be possessive, almost as much as I do, and I figure that Sophie had just triggered that in her.

I've been living the rockstar lifestyle hard, and I need a break. Something small like recording a few TikToks with Sophie might be just what I need.

"All right, I'm in the garage, come on over," I tell her and hang up.

She's there in an alarmingly short period of time, and I remember vaguely her saying that she lived close. *Very* close, it turns out, if she's able to get here this quickly.

I don't think much of it, smiling to greet her even though the sunlight streaming through the garage door while it opens feels like a knife stabbing through my eyeballs. *Fuck.* I have got to stop with all the tequila. I feel like hell, and I must look it, too because Sophie whistles.

"You must have tied one on last night," she giggles, and I give her a weak smile.

"You can say that again," I say dryly, and Sophie perches next to me on one of the old boxes in the garage. I'm sitting on a storage bin with my guitar hooked up to an amp and laid over my lap. I've been strumming it off and on, trying to find the right rhythm.

Sophie hums along with the melody, and her humming helps me find the right key.

"Thanks, Soph. I've been struggling with that all morning."

"Seems like you've been struggling a lot lately," Sophie says gently, and I groan in the back of my throat and laugh a little.

"Yeah, I guess you could say that." I look up and I'm shocked to see how close she's sitting, having leaned over, close enough that she could tilt forward just a bit and kiss me.

Do I want her to kiss me? Part of me just wants her to do it, to get it over with, so that maybe I can finally move on. I'm tired of the back and forth with Harley, of the will she/won't she every single day. Maybe if I let Sophie kiss me...

She leans forward, her eyes closing shut slowly, and I pull away, clearing my throat.

"Show me the footage you have of the concert," I say softly, and Sophie pouts only for a moment before perking up and scrolling through the footage on her phone.

Even if I think that kissing Sophie might get me a little further past my relationship with Harley, it isn't right to lead her on. Sophie is a nice girl, and I don't want to fuck her over. I'm not in the right head space to be kissing *anyone*, let alone someone new.

I fix up and post a few TikToks with her concert footage. I can't believe she'd been so close to the stage, and I hadn't seen her at all. I guess I'd been preoccupied for a long time now.

Sophie helps me a little more with the lyrics of my new song, and while listening to me sing it she tilts her head, looking at me quizzically.

"You really feel what you're singing, don't you?" she

asks, and I think that's probably the most interesting question I've been asked in my career.

I nod. "Yeah, I feel it all pretty hard," I laugh a little. "I guess that's not always a good thing."

"You're passionate," she insists. "That's sexy."

I look away from her and she chuckles softly.

"Don't worry. I know you're still hung up on your ex. If you ask me, she's still hung up on you, too."

My eyes shoot to hers. "Why do you say that?"

"She wanted to beat my ass the other night when I tried to kiss you. You were too drunk and not into it, so I just smiled at her, trying to make amends. She wasn't having it. I'm surprised she didn't take a swing at me."

I laugh. "Harley can be a spitfire."

Sophie nods. "That your kid that she's hauling around? That's probably why she was so grumpy, you know."

The reality of the situation washes down on me suddenly at her words, and I feel glum all over again, looking down at my guitar.

"Not mine," I say softly, and Sophie touches my upper arm.

"From what I can tell, *she* might be, though, Axel."

Sophie probably has no idea how much those simple words make me feel better, but I promise myself that I'll let her know. I want to be her friend since I can't be anything else to her. She's a good person, and without her, I'm not sure if I would have done so well the last few months. She keeps me focused on work, helps with my music, and she's a good friend to me.

Just like Gemma.

I figure it'll hurt Sophie if I tell her that I view her like a little sister, so I keep my mouth shut. Maybe if I stay focused on work, even after Sophie leaves, I can make things right with Harley again.

The way things turn out, I couldn't have been more wrong.

* * *

Harley doesn't come home that night, or the night after. I can't deny that I'm going a little crazy. I send her repeated text messages and leave her a voicemail, even though I'm not quite sure she doesn't still have me blocked.

Where could she be? I curse myself for not waiting to see where she'd gone and instead riding off on my motorcycle to the diner to drown my sorrows in pancakes and syrup. When she finally returns, I haven't had a drink in two days and I'm so sober it feels like the clarity of everything actually hurts.

It's a little frightening to imagine how little I've been actually sober in the last six months, better yet, ever since Harley and I split. I'm lucky I don't start having withdrawal symptoms.

She steps out of someone's car and I frown but when I get closer I can see Charlotte and her trademark red hair. I wave at her and she waves back genially enough.

Harley is frowning, lowering her head as she storms toward her side of the duplex.

"Harley," I start, my voice tired. I haven't been able to sleep at all the last two nights, wondering where she'd been. It seems like she's been with Charlotte, which makes me feel infinitely better, and I just want to make things right

"Leave me alone, Axel. I'm busy tonight," she mumbles, barely any fight in her, and that makes me worry.

As long as Harley's fighting, I know she still cares, but she just sounds tired, now.

"Busy doing what?" I ask. "I was going to finish up the crib—"

Harley slams the door of her duplex open after fumbling with the key.

"That's not your responsibility, Axel. The baby is none of your business."

I hold up my hands as if in defense. "Okay, okay. Sorry I give a shit, Harley."

"*Do* you? Do you *really* give a shit, Axel?" Harley spits at me, and I blink.

I didn't expect this type of vitriol from her, despite how we'd left things.

"Of course I do," I insist, but Harley's chin is tilted up and her blue eyes are full of fire.

"You didn't care before, when we were married. You'd come home at daylight smelling like tequila and your groupie whores and you didn't care about what I thought then, did you?"

"Harley, we've been over this. I never let any of them touch me, hell, even after we split up, I couldn't bring myself to sleep with anyone else!" I burst out, and Harley stares at me, narrowing her eyes.

"You're full of shit. You're trying to tell me that you didn't get laid for—"

"Eight months," I say dryly. "Not until I moved here, the first time you and I hooked up."

"That's...that's *bullshit*, Axel. With your sex drive? There's no way."

"I didn't want anyone else," I insist. "I still don't want anyone else. This isn't over for me, Harley. This will *never* be over for me."

"Oh yeah? So why didn't you even hesitate to sign those divorce papers when I gave them to you?"

"I did. I asked you if you were sure. If that was what you wanted. You said yes. I didn't want to sign them, but if that was what would make you happy, I would. I couldn't keep you tied to me when you didn't want to be. But sweetheart, it killed me to sign those papers, because this thing between us? My love for you? This will never end. It can't."

Blinking at me, tears streaming down her eyes, she turns from me and heads to her side of the duplex. Before she enters, she says the words that shatter my heart. "It is over." Before I can say anything else, she slams the door in my face.

I stare at her closed door for what seems like ten minutes before I let out a string of curses. I want to punch the wall again, or the brick this time, but I'd learned my lesson last time. My knuckles still ached from the injury, and I don't want to have to ask for her help to bandage them. Not now.

I'm *furious,* suddenly. She doesn't believe me? After she spread her legs for someone else maybe a month after we split up? That's rich, coming from her. And what is she so *busy* doing tonight, anyway? I swear if she leaves the house with that fucking guy...

I stay out in the garage, playing my guitar obnoxiously loud, unable to help myself. Harley peeks through the blinds a couple of times but she doesn't come storming outside, much to my annoyance.

I want her to be as mad as I am, want her to fight with me, but she's shutting me out. She's been shutting me out ever since we split up, and it hurts worse than the cruelest thing she could say to me.

Sure enough, in a couple of hours she comes out dressed

in a red sundress that's a little too small across the bust, her cleavage spilling out. She looks amazing, but the words stick in my throat when I want to tell her that.

She gets into the Beetle without even looking at me and I go up to the window.

"Where are you going dressed like that?" I blurt out, before I know what I'm saying. Panic rises in my throat.

"None of your business," she shoots back, but she doesn't roll up her window, and that's something.

I place my hands on her window, bracing myself. "I want it to be my business."

"Well, it's *not*. We're divorced, remember?"

I throw up my hands in frustration. "Yeah, you won't let me fucking forget. You and that baby bump!"

"It's not a baby bump," she says through gritted teeth. "It's a *baby*, a girl, actually, and she's mine."

"Who else's is she, Harley?" I ask, a dangerous tone in my voice. I'm right on the edge of snapping and I know it. I want to destroy the whole garage with my bare hands, I'm so angry.

"That's none of your fucking business, either," Harley spits. "Now *move*. I'll be late."

"Late for *what*, Harley?" I nearly yell, but she puts the car in reverse, backing up so that I stumble forward and almost fall. I let out a hoarse yell and that's when it happens.

I snap. Everything comes down around me like a crowd: the divorce, how hard Harley's eyes had been when she signed those papers. The way she'd glared at me when I first showed up at her house, after, how she'd kicked me out the next morning. The way she'd turned, holding her belly that was full of someone else's baby, a screaming reminder that she'd let someone else touch her, let someone else love her.

And now, who the hell knows where she's going? A date? To the father?

I kick around the boxes in the garage in a fury, throwing my guitar across so that it bangs against the wall. I don't care that it'll be expensive to fix or replace. I don't care about anything, a red rage flooding over my vision.

Pictures of Harley as a child spill out of some of the boxes, along with some old pictures of us as teenagers, and I want to rip them to pieces. It's just a reminder of a past that I'll never have again. Just a reminder of what I want and can't have, no matter how hard I try.

I simply can't hold it in anymore, and I destroy most of the garage, even kick over my motorcycle which is sitting on its kickstand.

When it's over, I sit down on one of the overturned crates, putting my face in my hand and trying to remember how to breathe normally.

Chapter 20

Harley

I had thought a lot about my last conversation with Axel and all Charlotte had told me. My thoughts kept coming back to the fact that he had signed those papers for me, not because he'd wanted to. Thing is, I had gone to a lawyer and asked for those papers to test him. I loved him and I wanted to see if he loved me back. I didn't really want a divorce, I had wanted him to fight for me, but he hadn't. I had been so sure he didn't love me anymore, that he wanted his freedom.

And to find out now that he was only giving me mine because that's what I had asked made me look at everything in a new light.

I had to talk to Axel, to apologize and say all the things I need to say.

But as Charlotte is about to pull up, I see a familiar little car coming out of my driveway, and as she passes us, I see the little blonde that Axel brought home the other night.

I grit my teeth, stiffening.

"Harley," Charlotte warns, and I give her a big, fake smile.

"Don't worry," I assure her. "Everything's fine."

Of course, everything is not even remotely fine, and I'm *boiling* inside. I tell myself not to talk to him, tell myself not even to *look* at him, but he keeps saying my name, keeps walking closer to me, and I can't help myself.

I know I was awful, and I'd been implying that I am going out on a date when I'm not, but I'm just so *mad*. I couldn't help myself from saying all the cruel things I had locked deep inside me.

The only place I'm going to is my parents' house for dinner, but I had let Axel believe something else. I know how much that will fuck with his head, and I feel so cruel. This isn't me. I wipe at my eyes as I pull up to my parents' place.

My mother has gone all out with the dinner, roasting a chicken with some small potatoes. I'm surprised to see carbs in the meal since she's normally against them. When we eat, she doesn't get any for herself, though, and gives me the side eye when I get a big portion.

I don't care. I need comfort, and if it comes in food, so be it. I can't have what I want, after all, which is to go to Axel and start sobbing in his arms, tell him how sorry I am for everything. While we were hooking up, everything seemed so much simpler. Now that we're fighting all the time and he's stopped letting me in, everything seems awful. And I know this time I'm to blame, because I've been all over the place while he has been nothing but caring to me, blonde girl or not.

What I'm feeling now is what it was like before he moved in, when we were split up. This is the heartbreak I felt then. My whole life, I've been in love with Axel Jermaine, and I can't just turn that on and off like a switch. My body still craves him, yes, and I've been telling myself that's the only reason we were hooking up, but I'm a liar.

I still love him, and I don't know what the hell to do about it. Because I want to make sure I do the best for my baby girl, but what if by keeping him away, I'm making things worse?

My father is supposedly going to apologize for the other night, that's why my mother had drawn me here, but he's nowhere to be found.

"Where's Dad?" I ask, my teeth gritted. I'm not looking forward to his apology, which will probably be something like, "I'm sorry, but." That's the only way my father ever apologizes.

"He should be here soon," my mother says, eyeing my sundress. "That dress is getting a little tight, don't you think?"

I shovel potatoes into my mouth. "I'm eating for two," I say, giving her a forced smile.

My mother would usually say something like "You know that doesn't mean you can eat all you want," and tell me how during her pregnancy with me she only gained eleven pounds, but today, I guess she sensed my bad mood. She shuts her mouth and takes a sip of wine.

I look at the wine longingly. I have never been as big a drinker as Axel, but I love a glass of wine with dinner, and it's been a long eight months without it. I figure tonight, I'm going to miss it more than ever.

My father comes in already looking a little disheveled, and I can smell whiskey on him. He must have stopped by the bar after work, something he does on occasion. I roll my eyes and Mom gives me a hard look.

"Harley," he greets, and I shut my mouth, pressing my

lips closed. I refuse to speak to him until I hear that apology. "*Harley,*" he says again, as if he's pressing me to speak, but I keep my mouth closed.

He sighs heavily and plops down a bit unsteadily in the chair at the head of the table. My mother begins spooning out chicken, vegetables, and potatoes for him. Funny how she fills his plate and judges me for filling mine.

"I'm sorry that you're mad at me," he starts, and that's hardly an apology, so I keep eating, ignoring him. "But you know that I only want what's best for you."

"And how, exactly, do you know what's best for me?" I ask, unable to keep my silence. "You barely speak to me unless it's to criticize me."

My father looks taken aback. To be fair, since I'd gotten pregnant, he'd been less absent, but it doesn't make up for a lifetime of him being in and out of my life.

"You're my *daughter*, Harley."

"I hope that I treat my daughter's decisions better than you've treated mine," I mumble, and my mother throws her napkin down on the table.

"Now, Harley, don't talk to your father that way," she hedges, and I frown at her.

"I'm not a teenager anymore, Mom. I can speak my mind."

"Not at my dinner table, you won't," she snaps back, and I push back from the table.

My father holds out a hand to stop me. "Wait, Harley." He pauses. "Please."

I don't get up, but I also don't scoot my chair back up. It will just be harder for me to leave angrily when I need to.

"Axel isn't right for you. I've told you that before," my father says, and my jaw tightens.

"Is Mom right for you? Or should it have been one of those affair partners of yours? Remember when I caught you out to dinner with Elena, my au pair?"

My father blanches. "Harley, that was years ago."

"I guess it's hard for me to forget. Do you know that's why it didn't work between me and Axel? I didn't trust him. Couldn't trust him. I wonder why." I sneer at him.

"Harley Eloise Telman," my mother says in a warning tone, but I don't care. I stand up from the table.

"Axel Jermaine never lifted a finger for you, Harley. We're the ones that helped you put down the deposit on this duplex. We're the ones who have been here for you all this time."

My eyes snap to my father's. "Oh, like the first year we were married, when Axel worked two jobs on top of performing with the Spades every weekend? He put me through college, because *you* cut me off when we got married. I got my English degree and he supported me. You told me my degree was useless."

"You're rich, You don't need a degree," my father drawls, as if that's a dirty word, something like scum beneath his shoe, and I glared at him.

"After he paid for me to get through four years of school, I thought the least I could do was help him by getting a job. Maybe I should have been more. Maybe I *would* have been more, if I had a family that supported me no matter what I chose."

"You chose *wrong*, Harley!" my father bellowed. "Axel comes from nothing and you—"

"I come from a home where my father would rather be getting his dick wet than coming home to see his daughter," I shoot back, and my mother gasps. "Axel was the only decision I ever made for myself. You two controlled everything in my life. You won't control me anymore, and you will not control this baby."

I put a hand on my stomach, something twinging deep in my abdomen. I wince as I storm out to the car, wondering if I should mention it to the doctor. She said that Braxton Hicks contractions were normal, but these that I've been having lately are intense.

On the way home, I think about what I said about Axel, how he supported me when we were first married. It's true, he did put me through college, and the only reason I'd steeled for the first job opening that had accepted me was to help him with his music. I resented that, but at the end of the day, he'd helped me and I'd helped him, like couples do. I'd also told my father that I hadn't trusted Axel, and that was true, too, although as far as I know, he was never unfaithful.

Have I let the damage my parents did to me color my reactions to him? Axel has never given me a reason not to trust him, yet I worried every time he came in late, every time a fan touched his arm on stage. Have I been wrong all this time?

I decide to talk to him, to tell him that maybe I've been wrong. Even if we can't be together anymore, maybe one day, we can be friends. Maybe one day, I can tell him about the baby, make him understand why I lied to him. I bite down on my bottom lip as I approach the house. There is a small U-Haul trailer in the driveway, one like Axel had moved in with.

I figure he's bringing in some new equipment for the band so I pull up next to the U-Haul, walking inside the garage.

Axel's bringing boxes out of his duplex and taking them to the trailer. He walks past me without speaking.

"What... what are you doing?" My heart has dropped somewhere among my toes, and I feel like I can barely breathe, my throat closing with panic.

"Moving out," he grunts, throwing the boxes with not much gentleness into the trailer and returning to his duplex for more.

I just stand in the middle of the garage, shell-shocked. "My father isn't buying the place, Axel. You don't have to do this."

Axel pauses, brushing off his pants where dust has gathered on some of the boxes. "Isn't this what you wanted?" He takes a few steps toward me, his blue eyes flashing with anger. "Didn't you want me gone?"

I nod slowly, thinking that's what I *used* to want.

Something different flashes across his face, something like hurt, but he shutters it up quickly, making his expression blank.

"Then I'm giving you what you want. Again," he said, his voice low and almost hoarse, and I wonder if he's been drinking or crying or both. His eyes look red-rimmed and a little bloodshot, but I don't smell tequila on him.

"Axel," I start, but he keeps moving. I just watch him, tears welling in my eyes, until he brings out one final box. He hands it to me, shoving it against my chest so that I fumble and drop it. A framed picture of us at our wedding falls to the garage floor and shatters.

Axel looks down at it for a moment before looking back up at me, searching my face and I don't know what he's searching for.

"Goodbye, Harley," he says, and puts on his helmet. He

gets on the motorcycle, slowly turning the wheel so that he can exit with the trailer through the yard.

I stand there, looking down at the shattered picture, and burst into tears.

Chapter 21

Axel

"Thanks for letting me stay here for a while," I say to Samuel, holding a bottle of tequila between my thighs on his couch.

Samuel arches an eyebrow. "Yeah, yeah, okay, just don't throw up on my floor this time, okay?"

"That was *one time*," I argue. It had been the first week after Harley served me divorce papers, so I think I should be forgiven based on the circumstances.

Samuel rubs a hand over the back of his neck. "Seriously, though, wake me if you need me, yeah?"

I nod, taking a swig from the bottle and wincing. It's a cheap bottle, cheaper than I'm used to, and it stings in the back of my throat. It numbs the edges of my mind and the ache in my heart, though, so it's doing its job.

Harley hasn't called, not that I expect her to. She hadn't called the whole time we'd been split up, despite my alcohol and regret-soaked voicemails and incoherent text messages. It doesn't matter what I do: it's over.

"Fuck," I mumble, running a hand across my face and Samuel looks at me.

142

"Are you sure you're okay to be alone?" he asks softly, and I think about it.

The truth is, I honestly don't know. It's not like I'm going to off myself, but after half a bottle of tequila I might get maudlin.

"Nah. I'll wake you up if I get all weepy," I promise with a weak grin. "I promise."

Samuel nods but he doesn't look convinced, trailing off to his bedroom after a few moments.

I look down at my phone, at her contact picture, which is one of her open mouthed, laughing, looking as beautiful as I've never seen her. I swallow hard, feeling like something's stuck in my throat. It feels like I don't have any tears left to give, and honestly, I don't know what I'm going to do next.

I could go out to a bar, but what happens there? We don't have a concert for another three days, with Gemma setting us up for a few gigs around the biggest cities in Arizona. I have nothing to occupy my time, and that can be bad when I feel like this.

I don't think I'd be any fun out, but the tequila starts to taste like maybe it might be a better idea than scrolling through pictures of Harley on my phone. I miss her, and not just her body, like she'd claimed. I miss her smile and her blue eyes and the way she'd loved me.

I sigh heavily, angrily wiping at my eyes, and schedule myself an Uber with one eye squeezed shut to keep my vision from doubling. I don't plan to remember the next few hours, so why not spend it out?

What's the worst that can happen?

* * *

I wake up eight hours later with my mouth so dry that I can barely get my lips apart. I'm in an unfamiliar bed, and I groan when I sit up, my head pounding. I'm not wearing a shirt, and it occurs to me that I should be worried that I slept with someone. From the state of me, though, I think it's unlikely.

"You threw up all over your clothes," the voice from the doorway says dryly.

I squint, looking up, to see Jackson standing there, leaning against the doorjamb.

"Did we hook up?" I ask jokingly, and Jackson barks out a laugh.

"Yeah, yeah, you were a real animal. You puked on my shoes, so you owe me a new pair." He points at me.

"Got it," I manage, trying to blink the sleep from my eyes. "Did I call you?"

"I went out to try to find you. Samuel was worried, said you'd downed half a fifth of tequila before you ever went out."

Jackson is no stranger to going off the rails, having his own period of time in which he could barely keep his shit together. I always suspected it was over some girl, the same way me going off the rails is because of Harley, but he wouldn't ever spill.

Jackson can be close-mouthed about his personal life, even to us guys, and I respect that. I don't have the same problem, though. Everyone knows about me and Harley by this point, and everyone knows I'm a mess over her. I look around for my phone but it's nowhere to be found, probably cracked on the ground in the alley outside the Dirty Dozen.

Jackson hands me a bottle of water.

"I could kiss you, Jack," I tell him, sucking half of it down.

"Please don't. I bet your breath smells like death," he complains, and it surprises me into a laugh. I almost spray water everywhere, suddenly feeling nauseous and dizzy. Jackson looks at me. "When's the last time you ate?"

My stomach grumbles as if reacting to his words. "Uh...I don't know. Sometime yesterday. Maybe the day before."

My appetite leaves me when I'm stressed, and I'd been extremely stressed ever since I moved in with Harley.

"Jesus," Jackson mumbles. "We need to get something on top of all that liquor. Stay here, I'll order us something."

I give him a weak smile. "My hero."

Jackson snorts and pulls out his phone. I can't care less what he orders, knowing that any food will look unappetizing until I ate it given the state of my hangover. Anything will help the feeling, but it'll be hard keeping it down at first.

"I feel like you're becoming way too familiar with hangovers," Jackson says, and I realize that I'd said some of that out loud.

I bark out a laugh that doesn't have much mirth in it. "Maybe. You know how it goes."

Jackson nods. "I do. And I know where it ends," he says softly.

I sigh, running my hands over my head. "I know. I know I need to get it together, Jack, but Harley..." I trail off as he tilts his head at me.

"What you've got to do is move on, Ax. You have to let her go."

"I can't," I say, looking away as my voice breaks. "That's the one thing I can't do."

Jackson sits with me for a moment, and he doesn't clown me for crying, thank God, just claps me on the

145

shoulder and heads off to the living room to give me some space.

When he returns, I've dried it up and he brings me a breakfast platter from the nearby diner. I get half of it down, at least, and start to feel a little more human.

"What happened?" Jackson asks finally, and I groan.

"Nothing. Everything. She just doesn't want me there. She's got the new baby and somebody else."

"Somebody else?"

"She went out on a date last night. I trashed the garage after she left. I can't stay there, man. I can't stay there and watch her go out on dates and have that baby.... it'll kill me," I admit.

"And you've told her how you feel? Or have you just told all of us," Jackson says dryly.

"She knows how I feel," I argue. "She knows that I love her."

"How? Because you've been fucking her lately?"

I rankle at that. "That's not what I mean. I've told her that I love her."

"After you fucked her?" Jackson asks, and I sigh.

"Why does that matter?"

Jackson rolls his eyes. "C'mon, man. After all this time, you don't understand women?"

"I've only ever been with Harley and one other girl," I admit, my face flushing a little.

Jackson gapes at me. "*What*? You *must* still be drunk."

"I'm serious," I admit. "There was one girl before Harley, and ever since I met her, I haven't even been able to look at anyone else."

"Jesus Christ. All that time on tour, and you-"

"Not once," I admit. "Although there were a few times I got close. They just felt wrong, you know?"

Jackson presses his lips together like he knows exactly what I'm talking about, but I don't pry even though I'm curious.

"And you've told her that?"

"She doesn't believe me," I say glumly.

"Hell, *I* don't believe you," Jackson laughs. "But you better have your shit together before the Santa Fe concert."

"Yeah, yeah. Music first, I know," I say, and Jackson shakes his head.

"Nah. Music is second next to family, but right now, it's what you need."

Jackson's right, and I know it. There's nothing to do but go on with my life, no matter how much it hurts. I've got to put away the tequila and get over Harley Telman. I don't have much faith that I will, given that it's been nearly nine months since our divorce, and I can't let it go.

I have to try. Step one is getting rid of the tequila. Step two is trying to stop thinking about who she might have gone on that date with. The father? That fucking guy who kept showing up to pick her up for work?

I tell myself it doesn't matter, that I need to stop thinking about how I know where she works, how I could blow it all up. I could tell the guy that I'm her ex, that we've fucked three times now. I could end it, ruin her relationship just to be petty and spiteful. Funny thing is, I'm thinking this (moderately) sober instead of drunk, and that almost convinces me to do it.

It's not like I think it's a good idea. At the very least it'll blow up everything between me and Harley, but what does it matter if it's over anyway? What else do I have to lose?

"Your dignity," Jackson says when I tell him my plan, and I grin at him.

147

"Bold of you to assume I ever had any to begin with when it comes to Harley Telman-Jermaine."

Jackson rolls his eyes. "All right. Well, unhook your trailer or whatever before you make an ass of yourself. I'll meet you at the Dozen later."

The lead singer of the band looks tired, bags under his eyes, and I tilt my head.

"Is something going on with you, Jackson?"

Jackson rubs his hand across his face. "You could say that," he mutters but doesn't offer any more and I don't push.

After all, he's enabling me to do maybe the most impulsive and stupid thing I've ever done.

That's what real friends are for.

Chapter 22

Harley

So, it's over. After a dozen years of my life being in love with Axel Jermaine, he's done with me, and it is all my fault. He's moved out of the duplex, and he doesn't answer my calls all night. I only call him twice, to be fair, but it goes straight to voicemail.

I almost call in to work the next morning, my eyes puffy from crying all night and exhausted from not sleeping, but in the end, I decide to go. I need to get my life back to normal before this baby is born, and this is the way to do it.

I put on some light makeup and a maxi dress that contains the baby bump to some degree, although it's hard to do that at this stage in my pregnancy. My mother would probably have something to say about it.

I get a call from Theresa on my morning break.

"Did you know someone's trying to buy the duplex?" she asks as soon as I answer the phone.

I sigh heavily. "Yeah, my father. Can I ask you not to sell it to him? At least until you find me something else?"

Theresa lets out a long breath. "It's not up to me, Harls. He's buying it from the company, not from me, but I can

149

stall the escrow for a bit. I've got a two-bedroom coming up in a couple of weeks."

That will be cutting it pretty close with the birth of the baby, but what else can I do?

"Thanks. Please put me on the list."

"Are you... are you doing okay, Harley?"

Tears spring to my eyes at the question. *Stupid hormones,* I think to myself for about the four hundredth time this month.

"I'll be okay, Theresa. We should do dinner soon."

"Absolutely! How about Saturday?"

We chat for just a few moments more before I hang up, and I find myself grateful that I've connected with her and reconnected with Charlotte. I need people in my life, people who aren't my parents or Axel, even if I've been trying to push everyone away. Charlotte is the only one who knows my secret, and I know that she won't tell.

Part of me has been considering telling Axel, seeing what his reaction is, but after he's moved out without warning, I think it might be bad timing. If I tell him now, it might seem like a desperate attempt to get him back. I'm going right back around to the same thoughts, how I don't want him to choose me because of the baby.

I want him to choose me because he wants *me.* And for more than just sex. But the first time he thinks I might be seeing someone else, he runs. What does that say about us? Nothing good. We had always both been possessive, but running at the first sign of trouble doesn't bode well. If he doesn't want me and this baby now, why would he if he knew it was his?

I frown down at my empty lunchbox. Roland, who works in the office beside mine, comes up to the my desk.

"You hungry?" he asks, and I can't help but nod. I'm

starving, the baby's kicking around and craving sushi that I can't have because of the raw fish. I could make do with some salmon, though.

He gives me a half smile and I realize once again that Roland really *is* attractive. He's clean-cut, different in nearly every way than Axel is, but he's a handsome guy. Not really my type, though.

My type is one Axel Jermaine, and that's something I need to work on. I guess that's why I say yes to Roland's lunch invitation, even though I make it clear that it's a co-workers and friends only date.

Roland laughs and holds up his hands. "Fair enough. No funny business." He winks at me and I blush a little as we exit the building.

Our boss, Sheila, can be kind of a hound about us getting back on time and she's leaving the office at the same time, so I'm trying to hurry, waddling along behind Roland.

He pauses to wait for me, and that's when I hear the sound of the motorcycle roaring up to the building, parking in a no-parking zone with red sighs.

No, I tell myself. *It can't be.*

But I'd know Axel's flame covered helmet anywhere, and I just focus on Roland's car, trying to get there before he catches sight of me.

"Hey!" he calls, pulling his helmet off and grinning. It doesn't have much mirth in it, though, seeming almost fake, and I stop in my tracks. Roland looks at me, tilting his head in confusion, and I give him an apologetic smile.

Axel walks up to me, still giving me that fake grin.

"What the hell are you doing here?" I hiss, and he shrugs,

"Haven't seen the place where you work in a while. Maybe I was curious."

Roland walks up behind me and I squeeze my eyes shut, expecting nothing good to come out of this.

"Who's this?" Roland asks, and I grit my teeth.

"Her husband," Axel replies.

"*Ex-husband*," I say through gritted teeth, and Roland frowns.

"Huh. Well, we were just about to go to lunch. Would you like to join us?"

Bless Roland, he can be so sweet and calm, but his jaw is tight and he reaches down to take my hand, hoping to comfort me, maybe. I'm not sure why he did it, but looking back, I think that's where it all fell apart.

Axel looks down at our hands, and there's a muscle twitching in his jaw. "Are you the one that knocked her up?"

I gasp at the crass way he asks, out on the street where my boss is still trailing behind us.

"I don't think that's any of your business," Roland says tightly, and keeps my hand tight in his even when I try to pull away.

"As her husband, I think it's very well my business," Axel growls, all sign of that fake grin dropping from his face. His blue eyes look bloodshot and wild, and my breath catches in my throat.

"Axel, don't!" I cry out, but it's too late, he shoves Roland right in the middle of the chest, and I stumble backward when he's forced to release my hands.

Roland, who I've always thought of as sweet and meek, doesn't back down, pushing Axel back. Axel stumbles off a curb and into the street.

"Axel, *stop!*" I yell, but I can't stop it, it's too late.

Axel throws a right hook and Roland goes down. Axel

straddles him immediately, punching him in the face, and I scream.

Sheila has her phone out, calling the cops, and I'm just crying and yelling.

I pull at Axel's shoulders, my nails digging into his shoulders, and finally, he stops. Roland gasps in a breath, his nose spurting blood, but he must be okay because he sits up.

My eyes are on Axel, who's bloody from Roland's injury and... *smiling*?

"This is what you wanted, right?" Axel asks me in a hoarse voice. "You wanted me to act like the unhinged rockstar you've always believed me to be? You wanted me to blow it all up? There you go, Harley. You're welcome."

I open my mouth to speak but I can't get a single word out as the cops pull up to my workplace. Axel raises his hands and hits his knees like he's done this before and my eyes widen as I stare at him in shock.

After that, the day goes by in a blur. I refuse to press charges, and so does Roland, when he looks at me sideways, and I'm sobbing at the back of a police car watching them haul Axel away.

Sheila tells me to go home, that we'll talk about this later, but I already know I won't be able to keep my job. I guess it doesn't matter. With no job, no friends, and no family, since my parents aren't talking to me, I have nothing and no one but this baby in my stomach.

Just the way I wanted it.

Chapter 23

Axel

I'm surprised that the square Harley chose caught me just above the eye and it's bleeding like a son of a bitch as I sit in my cell.

"Can I get a napkin or something?" I call, but they all ignore me. I groan and sit back down next to the drunk in the corner of the cell who smells like malt liquor.

"Get in a fight?" he slurs.

"Fell down some fist-shaped stairs," I joke, and lean back against the bars, sighing.

This is the second time I've been arrested in a year, so I guess I'm gonna have to get used to it. I'll have to spend the night here, most likely, and then I'll bite the bullet and call Samuel or Jackson...

"Jermaine! Release!" Someone shouts down the corridor after about six hours, and I stand up, confused.

When I make it out of processing, the whole band is standing around outside, including Gemma who sticks her head out of the big van she'd bought to haul us all around and narrows her pretty green eyes at me.

"Get in," she snaps, and Locke shakes his head, laughing a little.

"Shut up," I mutter. "Last time was your fault, so you owed me one."

He holds up his hands in defense, grinning, and Samuel gives me a wry look from the very back seat.

"Are me and Gemma the only ones without an arrest record?" he asks, and Gemma clears her throat.

Jackson bursts out laughing and Locke frowns.

"You've been arrested, little bit?"

Gemma shrugs. "Once."

"Underage drinking," Jackson says, giggling. "She snuck into one of my frat parties during my one semester of college and got caught by the fuzz."

Samuel rolls his eyes. "I'm friends with a bunch of criminals."

"Don't worry, Sammy. We'll pop your cherry yet," Jackson says, ruffling his hair, and Samuel blushes but he's smiling.

"Your charges were dropped, but the state might bring some. The office manager was pretty pissed it happened at the building," Gemma says.

I groan. "Yeah, I'll definitely catch a fine, at least."

It's over, now. Really over, and I blew it all up myself, just like she always believed I would.

"You guys are lucky that your antics make our fans laugh," Gemma huffs. "You really embody the rockstar lifestyle."

"Except for me!" Sam pops up proudly, and Gemma looks into the rearview mirror as she's pulling out and smiles softly at him.

"Except for you, Sammy "

Locke rankles a bit in the front seat. He hates it anytime

Gemma gives any of us attention, and I can't help but chuckle under my breath. Too bad I'm too heartbroken to flirt with her myself.

Locke hands me a bunch of napkins and even though the blood has dried up, I dab at my face a little, hissing when it stings.

"What happened?" Gemma asks.

"Harley," Jackson answers dryly, and Gemma rolls her eyes.

"*Obviously*. But what?"

I shrug. "Her new boyfriend gave me attitude."

Jackson snorts. "You planned for him to give you attitude."

"I just knew he would," I respond defensively and Gemma pulls into a local burger joint with a squeal.

"Axel Thomas Jermaine," she says, bringing out my dreaded middle name and everything. "You started a fight?"

"Yes, Mom. I'm sorry," I joke, but she's not having it, her green eyes flashing.

"You *idiot*! How are you supposed to get her back now?" she all but yells.

"I thought you told me to move on!" I cry, and she groans and shakes her head.

"Women never say what they mean," Locke says sagely, and Gemma hits him on the shoulder.

"I told you that because you *never* listen, Axel. I knew you'd do some dumb shit to get her back but this is going in the wrong direction! You've been a mess the past nine months because of this girl and you just go and blow it all up?"

"She's having someone else's baby," I say glumly. "And she doesn't want me. She left me. What am I supposed to do?"

"If she asked you to come back right now, baby and all, would you do it?" Gemma's turned around at the steering wheel now, glaring at me in person instead of through the rearview mirror.

The guys are silent, save Samuel who's trying to stop from snickering in the backseat.

I look down at my hands in my lap, nodding. It's embarrassing, that I'd take her back after everything, but I would.

"Then I'm taking you to go talk to her," Gemma says determinedly, and I rub my hands across my face.

"Can we stop somewhere so I can clean up first?" I ask.

"No," she says stubbornly, and true to her word when I give her the address, she drives me to Harley's duplex, the place where I had lived up until the night before.

I have no idea what I'm even going to say, but I guess I've got to figure it out because Gemma drops me off at the duplex and drives away while the guys try to keep their laughter in so they won't face her wrath.

Harley's Beetle is in the garage, at least, so I know she's home. I sigh and look in the window of the empty side of the duplex that used to be mine. I look like shit, hungover and with blood drying down one half of my face, but there's nothing to be done about it. I've already turned in the key to the duplex to the real estate office.

I approach the door slowly and I hear the click of the lock before I even lift my hand to knock.

Harley's standing there, dried tear tracks down her face and her pregnant belly bulging against her maxi dress and I feel like shit for making her cry.

"Harley," I say, but then I can't think of anything to make things better

"I lost my job," she says hoarsely. "My parents won't talk to me."

My heart aches. "Harley, let me help you," I start, and she cuts me off.

"I don't need your kind of help, Axel. You did this. What am I supposed to do now?" she begins to cry, and I think she'll kick me out, push me off the front step, but instead, she walks into my arms, pressing her forehead against my chest. "You idiot. You *asshole*."

"I'm sorry," I say softly, but I'm not. I'm not sorry at all if it makes her come into my arms like this, crying and vulnerable. Maybe that makes me a bad person, but I can't help it. I just want Harley, any way I can get her, and I don't care if this is what it takes. "I love you," I finish, and that's more true, more genuine, than my apology.

"Do you?" Harley asks, lifting her head to look at me with liquid blue eyes. "Do you really, Axel?"

Instead of answering, instead of telling her the same thing I've been telling her over and over since we split, I duck my head to kiss her, softly, just lightly brushing my mouth against hers.

Harley makes a sound in the back of her throat, her arms going around my neck and it's a repeat, my favorite rerun. She melts against me, pressing her mouth against mine harder than I had, more insistent. Her tongue slips through my lips and I'm already hardening in my jeans.

I rock my hips against her to show her. "You feel what you do to me, sweetheart? I always want you. Every moment of every day," I rasp, my voice hoarse from drinking the night before and lack of sleep for the past few weeks.

"I always want you, too," Harley admits in a small voice, and she seems small in my arms despite her belly, seems fragile, somehow.

I crouch to scoop her up, bridal style, and she squeaks.

"You can't pick me up," she insists. "I'm too heavy,

now."

I carry her easily to the bedroom, lie her down on the bed. "Light as a feather," I joke, although she does weigh more than she did before, it doesn't bother me. I lift more than her body weight every other day at the gym.

I kiss down her throat, leaving a mark at the base of her throat right next to another fading one that I'd left before. I want to mark her all over, leave a purple necklace of marks so that everyone knows that she's mine, but I contain myself.

I slide my hands down her maxi dress, and she protests when I try to pull it over her head.

"Axel, no, I don't... I don't look like I used to," she says, looking away from me, and I frown.

Her belly has stretched out her skin slightly, leaving little marks, and there's a dark line beneath her belly button, and her breasts are larger, seeming swollen, but other than that, she's still the same Harley I married.

"You're beautiful," I tell her, and I mean it. It doesn't matter that she's pregnant, even though something still rolls in my stomach every time I think about it. It doesn't matter who the father is, because she's still mine, and anything that comes from her will be part of her, and be mine too.

I want to tell her that, want to tell her everything, but her back is arching while my hands palm across her nipples, her breath coming shorter. She's been so sensitive while she's been pregnant, and I have to admit that I like it, how easy it is to make her come.

I slide my fingers down beneath her panties to slip my thumb across her swollen clit, and she cries out my name, rocking against my hand.

"Axel," she begs, "please. Want you inside me. Now."

There's something firm in her voice that makes me chuckle low in my throat.

"But I love the way you look when you come around my fingers, sweetheart," I murmur, looking down at her when I slip two fingers inside, curling them up just the way she likes. She gasps loudly, holding her breath, and I know that means she's close. She always holds her breath when she's just about to go over the edge.

"I'm going to—" she starts, and holds her breath again.

I grin at her before turning my eyes back to where I'm pumping my fingers in and out of her slowly and then faster as she whines. She finally releases her breath in a burst when she begins to clench around my fingers, her inner thighs trembling.

"Axel," she moans. "Axel, Axel, Axel."

My name on her lips makes an ache shoot through my cock, and I'm so ready to be inside her that I fumble with the button of my jeans. She whimpers, almost like she's going to cry again, when I get onto the bed instead of spearing into her. I don't want to hurt her, and her belly is in the way too much for missionary, but I have an idea.

I sit with my back against the headboard and pull her up into a sitting position. She frowns at me, and I just smile back at her.

"Miss how you ride me," I tell her, and her eyes go dark with lust.

She pouts. "I can't, with the baby," she starts, and then I tug her back toward me, resting her back against my chest, my dick pressing into her back.

"Oh," she says in wonder. "*Oh.*" She shifts her hips so that she can guide me inside, slowly, and I grit my teeth not to buck up beneath her.

I reach my hands around to cup her breasts, thumbing across her nipples and she moans low in the back of her throat, almost animal sounding, when she starts to roll her hips. I match her moans with my own, feeling like I'm close to bursting already with the way she tightens around me.

She rolls her hips back and forth and I take hold of her hips in my hand, bouncing her gently. It's not fast and hard like usual, not feral like we usually fuck, but I can kiss the side of her neck, leave marks along her shoulders.

Harley turns her head to kiss me and my head spins. This is different, somehow, more intimate than it has been. It makes me want to burst inside her right away, how close we are, how her mouth is soft and sweet against mine.

I reach around our bodies, under her pregnant belly, to thumb across her clit and she cries out, clenching around me, coming again so soon after her first orgasm. I don't want this to be over. I don't want her to come down from her orgasms and suddenly kick me out, tell me I've ruined her life, but I can't help it. My orgasm's approaching like a freight train and I dig my fingers into her hips, thrusting up into her hard and fast.

Harley moans low in the back of her throat, her thighs trembling, and when I spill inside her I bite down on her shoulder and she sighs, as if satisfied with the bite.

I let a long breath out against her skin, licking my teeth marks. As the lust fades, I start to feel down, waiting for her to push me away, climb off me and tell me to leave and never come back.

Instead, Harley leans back against me, nuzzles against the side of my face.

"Harley," I say softly, and she hums in the back of her throat. "What are we going to do now?"

She pauses, sighs heavily. "I don't know."

I swallow hard, squeeze my eyes shut, and press another kiss against her shoulder.

Here goes nothing.

Chapter 24

Harley

Axel is breathing hard, his chest heaving against my back. I turn to look at him to ask him if he's okay but his eyes are shut, his face furrowed.

"Axel?" I call, and he licks his lips, his eyes popping open.

He picks me up, hissing a little as he slips out of me, and deposits me on the bed next to him. I feel a twinge in my stomach, the baby kicking me in the ribs, and I wince.

Axel doesn't seem to notice, his eyes still shut.

"Axel?" I call again, and his eyes pop open, blue and bloodshot. He looks as if he hasn't been sleeping, or drinking too much, or both.

"Harley," he answers, and then shuts his mouth, rubbing a hand over his face.

I smile a little, propping myself up on one elbow, my belly lying on the bed next to me. The baby's still kicking in strange ways, and it's a bit uncomfortable.

"Cat got your tongue?" I tease, and Axel pouts just slightly. He's so handsome, even without sleep, and his hair is growing back in nicely. When we met, it was long and dirty blonde, almost as long as Jackson's. He'd shaved it just a few months into our marriage, and he looked just as good that way, but I am glad it is growing back a little.

"You know that I love you," he tells me, and I nod, sighing slightly and leaning back against the pillows. I rub my belly to try to get the baby to move out of my ribcage. "You know that I want you back," he continues, and I nod again.

"I do," I assure him, because even with the nod, he seems nervous, hesitant somehow. That's not like Axel. He wears his heart on his sleeve, especially with me, and he doesn't keep quiet hardly ever.

I lean against his shoulder, feeling sleepy, and he puts an arm around me. I expect him to continue talking, to tell me whatever it is he's been trying to tell me, but my eyelids feel so heavy. I suddenly feel tired, and these waves of exhaustion have been happening more and more often. I suppose it must be the baby. I expect Axel to keep talking, to tell me whatever it is he was going to tell me, but instead he's quiet and I drift off to sleep.

* * *

When I wake, I'm bitterly disappointed to reach over and find the bed empty. I sigh, rolling over onto my back before slowly sitting up on the side of the bed. I rub at my eyes, hoping that tears don't start to fill them before I even wake up properly. I can blame it on the hormones all I want, but the truth is that I want Axel with me. When I wake up, I want to be able to roll over and throw my arm over his waist, nuzzle into his throat.

I want Axel, but I might have messed everything up. He's gone and who knows where to. It's not like he lives next door to me anymore.

I stand up with a little difficulty, the bottom of my stomach feeling taut and painful. I plan to run myself a hot bath to try and soothe the pain, but I need a glass of water first. I slide on one of Axel's old t-shirts and manage to pull on a pair of sweats.

As I walk into the living room to get to the kitchen, I'm shocked to notice Axel sitting on the floor in front of a fully assembled crib.

He turns and smiles up at me, and *that's* when the tears come, streaming down my face before I can stop them.

"Harley," he calls, scrambling up from the floor. "Don't cry, sweetheart."

"Axel, you didn't have to—" I start, but he interrupts me.

"I did have to," he says firmly, taking my hands in his. "Because here's the thing, Harley. I want you, and you know that. But I don't care about the baby."

I cast my eyes down. "I know," I say softly, sniffling, and Axel makes a frustrated sound in the back of his throat.

"No, that's not what I meant! I mean, I don't care that you're pregnant with someone else's baby. I don't care who the father is. I want you *anyway*, Harley. I want you *and* the baby, because it'll be a part of you. I want everything with you, and just because we went a little off-course with how we started a family doesn't mean that I don't want it."

Axel takes my hands in his, sliding his thumb across my knuckles.

I look up at him, shocked. "You mean... even with the baby, you want to get back together? Are you sure?"

Axel nods. "Yes. Yes, Harley, I want to marry you again,

and it doesn't matter what happened while we were split. I can love you and this baby more than you can ever imagine."

I blink, tears still streaming down my face. This is what I want. This is *exactly* what I want, and I don't even know what to say. I guess I should start with telling him the truth and hoping that he doesn't hate me too much.

I had everything so mixed up, before. I kept thinking that Axel would never want me like this, that his love had conditions, but over the past few weeks I realize that Axel loves me *unconditionally*. Even though he thinks that I'm carrying another man's baby, he forgives me, and he loves me anyway.

That's more important than any of the petty reasons that I split up with him: he's a rockstar, girls are all over him, he might not be faithful. If Axel is willing to take me back even with everything I've put him through, it means that he's more faithful than I ever imagined.

I open my mouth to tell him and a sharp pain rips through my lower abdomen, radiating through to my lower back. I cry out, and I would have fallen if Axel wasn't holding my hands. He moves to wrap his arms around me and hold me up, looking down into my face.

My vision is blurry from the pain, ripping through in waves through my abdomen, and I manage a grunt before my knees buckle.

"Harley!" Axel cries, and I try to make words but my throat feels tight with panic when I look down at my sweatpants.

They're covered in red, too much red.

"Axel," I gasp out. "Tell them to save the baby. It's yours."

His face goes blank in shock, and the last thing I remember is him scooping me up in his arms before I pass out.

Chapter 25

Axel

N o. No no no no. That's all I'm thinking as I scoop Harley up and take her to the Beetle outside, getting her in the backseat before I curse, realizing that I don't have the keys.

I run back inside and thank God, they're in her purse, because I don't have time to waste. Harley's hurt, she's *bleeding* and the last thing she said had been crazy. It's crazy, there's no way that the baby is mine, so she must be really out of it.

I can't think straight, just focused on getting her there, and I nearly miss the turn three times.

I keep talking to her on the way, humming a few bars of songs to try and comfort her but she's dead silent and unconscious and I can't think about that too much or I'll panic. The panic is already close, rising in my stomach and chest, and if I give in I'll never get her to the hospital.

They wheel her in on a stretcher and the nurse ask me all kinds of questions: her blood type, her name, how far along she is. I can answer all the questions but that last.

"Are you the father?" The nurse asks, and I freeze as I'm following Harley into the back of the hospital.

"Yes," I choke out, because I'm doing the math in my fucked-up head and it's true, it has to be. If Harley's in labor now, she must have lied to me about how far along she was. It might be pre-term labor, but—she told me. It's mine.

"You have to wait here," the nurse says gently, and leads me to a chair in the waiting room. I watch Harley until the double doors close behind her.

When she's out of sight, my knees give out and I plop down in the chair, shell-shocked. Harley's having a baby, and it's *mine*.

I'm fucking *terrified*. Harley's bleeding and that doesn't seem normal.

And I'm going to be a father. Not just a stepfather, either.

I pull my phone out of my pocket and call the only person I can think of that will help.

"Gemma?" my voice breaks as soon as she answers the phone. "I'm at Lincoln Presbyterian. Can you come?"

* * *

The whole crew shows up instead of just Gemma. Locke, Jackson, and Sam crowd around me for a group hug while Gemma tries to get information at the front desk.

"He's her husband, you can tell him!" she insists, and thank God, Harley hasn't changed me as her emergency contact.

While Gemma gets all the information, Locke tilts his head in my direction.

"I'm not gonna ask if you're okay, because I know you're not," he says firmly. "Our time is coming and it fucking terrifies me. I can't even imagine what you are going through and I only hope I never have to. But we are here for you, brother. Always. Whatever you need."

"She...she told me the baby is mine," I manage, rubbing a hand across the back of my neck. "I'm going to be a father, Locke."

Locke's eyes widen but he doesn't react further. "I always thought the timing added up a little too well."

I stare at him. "What, you suspected?"

Locke shrugs. "Gemma and I talked about it. There's only a month difference, and it just seemed too convenient."

"So...she'd be month later? Maybe she's not pre-term?" I ask hopefully. I know from my sister that pre-term labor is more dangerous, and I want Harley and our baby to have the best chance they can.

I know, somewhere, that I should be angry with her, that I should be *furious* that she kept this from me, all this time, not to mention making me think she had been with someone else. But I can't bring myself to be anything but scared shitless that something will happen to her and our baby.

"She's not pre-term," Gemma says, coming back to sit across from me. "She's full-term, but the baby's breech."

"Upside down," Locke provides hopefully. "They told us about it in our last ultrasound."

"What does that mean for Harley?" I ask Gemma, biting at my lower lip nervously.

"They'll have to do a c-section," she says, and gives me a forced smile. "They do them all the time, it'll be fine."

There's something behind her eyes, something that seems off, and I stare at her.

"Something's wrong," I say, and stand up, looking around for the doctor.

169

Gemma stands up, puts a hand on my arm. "Axel, sit down. It's just...she's bleeding. Too much. Hemorrhaging. They're doing everything they can."

I sit down hard in the chair. "And the baby?"

"They're working on her," Gemma says. "The doctor says she's doing well."

"She?" I pause, tears springing to my eyes. "It's a little girl?"

Gemma smiles at me, keeping her hand on my arm. "You can see her soon, if you want to."

See her. I could see my daughter, brand new, while my wife was bleeding out on a table somewhere.

"No," I say, my voice cracking. "I'll wait until Harley can see her. We can see her together."

Gemma and Locke exchange a look, one of those only reserved for couples, but I squeeze my eyes shut. There's no way that Harley could be hurt. I won't accept it. She's going to be okay, and so is the baby, and that's that. I can tear her a new one for scaring me to death and lying to me about our baby.

There's plenty of fights to still be had.

Four hours and three cups of coffee later, I'm shaking as I stand in the nursery. The nurse touches my hand to get my attention, and I look around to see if I can recognize my baby among all the other infants. They all look the same, most of them sleeping, some of them fussing. There's only one that's crying, bawling, really, screaming her little lungs out, and that's the one that they bring me.

"You've got some pipes," I tell her as she nuzzles against me, rooting around and looking for something I can't give her. She quiets when the nurse adjusts her in my arms, but her little face is still all scrunched up. "Miss your mama, don't you?" I murmur. "Me, too."

She makes a little grunt and takes her fist to wrap around my thumb.

I think that maybe I'll die before I let the nurse take her back from me, but in the end, I let her go, and it's like the nurse is taking my heart with her when she wheels her back into the nursery.

I've never loved anything more than I love that little girl in that moment, and I know that no matter what happens, I'll protect her with my life. Just like I'll protect Harley.

The doctor comes out to talk to me right after I return from the nursery.

"She's lost a lot of blood," he says, and I nod numbly, feeling my face turn pale.

"Will she be all right?"

The doctor looks at me. "I don't know. We've given her a transfusion, and the bleeding has stopped. We just have to wait for her to wake up. It's up to her now."

I nod again, not knowing how else to respond to the news that the woman I've loved my whole life might never wake up. I get up to go outside and get some air.

I don't break down until I get out in the alley behind the hospital, and it's Samuel who follows me, my best friend in the Spades.

"She's going to be all right," I tell him through sobs, and he just hugs me tight.

"I know, Ax. I know."

She has to be. They both have to be okay, because it's the only way I'll ever be okay again.

Chapter 26

Harley

Axel doesn't want. He found someone else, brought home a girl that looks nothing like me.

"It's over, Harley," he tells me softly. He's not angry. Angry would mean that he cares. Angry would mean that he would fight for me. "It's just over."

I'm crying and holding my stomach and everything hurts and all I want is for him to take me into his arms.

"We tried as hard as we could," he says, and that's not Axel. That's not my Axel, he'd never give up like that.

"What are you talking about, Axel? You said you wanted me back, you said it didn't matter if I was pregnant—"

"That was before you lied to me, Harley. That was before you ruined everything."

"Axel," I choke out. "Axel, please." My throat feels tight, like something's stuck in it, and something's wrong. Something's horribly wrong because when I put my hands down to cradle my belly, my stomach is nearly flat.

Axel's holding a baby in his arms, suddenly, when he wasn't before, and the girl next to him, the same girl that was

172

in the garage trying to kiss him, kisses the baby on the top of the head.

"I'll take care of her," Axel promises, and I cry out, holding out my arms, but he's gone. I'm still in the duplex where everything ended, and I can see the crib he built standing tall and empty in the corner of the room.

There is darkness then, and I fight my way to the light but I'm barely conscious, in and out, when doctors and nurses come in and out of the room.

"Lots of blood," I hear someone say.

"She went through several pints of O neg," someone else says, a woman's voice. Nothing I recognize.

I wonder, briefly, if anyone has called my parents, and then realize it doesn't matter. It doesn't matter because the only person I want to be by my side is Axel.

"Axel," I murmur, but no sound comes out. It's like I'm a ghost, floating outside my body, but I can still feel every ache and pain. I feel empty in a way that makes me panic.

Where's my baby? I think, trying to speak it, but I can't, drifting off into nothingness.

* * *

When I wake up, I feel disoriented and groggy, and so weak it's like I can barely stick my tongue out to wet my dry lips. No one is in the room with me and getting to the nurse's button seems like a Herculean effort, but I manage.

The nurse's eyes widen when she comes to the room.

"Where's my baby?" I demand, and she skirts out of the room like I've said there was a fire. Doctors come around me, crowding my space and checking my monitors, but eventually, I'm told that I lost a lot of blood during surgery and delivery, and that I'm lucky to be alive.

"I already know I'm lucky," I croak, trying to joke. "But I want to see my baby. How is she?"

"She's doing well," the doctor assures me. I'd gone to such lengths to secure a good ob-gyn, but it ended up that my baby was delivered by a stranger. I suppose he must have done a good job, since we were both okay, within reason. "But someone else has been asking for you."

When Axel enters the room with our baby, something jumps into my throat, and tears burst from my eyes. I'd cried throughout my whole pregnancy, because I was alone and things seemed hard, not just the hormones. Now, I'm crying because I've never been so happy to see Axel grinning ear to ear.

"She looks just like you," Axel says, but when I look at our baby she has his nose and chin, so obviously, I snort out a laugh.

"Other way around," I insist, my voice still cracked and hoarse.

Axel kneels next to me, so that I can smell the baby's fresh scent on the top of her head.

"She's really mine?" Axel asks, and I freeze for a moment before I realize that I've already told him.

"She's yours," I insist, and God, it feels good to get it off my chest, feels like there's something heavy and awful lifting from my shoulders.

"You lied to me," Axel accuses, and I think of what I know now was dream Axel saying, *"It's just over, Harley,"* and I wonder if that's what's about to happen, if he's about to tell me it's over, that we tried hard enough.

"I know," I choke out. "I'm sorry."

"All this time, I could have been going with you to ultrasounds, I could have..." Axel's voice breaks and the baby coos, as if comforting him. It makes me crack a smile through my tears.

I stroke his hair awkwardly, reaching over the baby. I haven't even thought about names, not once. I've been so occupied with everything else that I've been neglecting things. I've been neglecting *myself,* and I could kick myself for not keeping a better eye on my pregnancy symptoms.

"It's my fault," I agree. "I was wrong."

Axel looks up at me, sniffling. He's crying, which isn't unusual after a fight, but this time, there's something full of pain in his face.

"You *were* wrong. You shouldn't have lied to me," he insists. "I missed so much. For both of you. I could have been there for you, Harley! I could have—"

I shush him, biting my lip as I ask him the only question that matters.

"Will you be here now, Axel?"

Axel looks at me, tilting his head and looking down at the baby, and slowly, he smiles.

"Of course I will be. I'll be here for anything this little girl needs."

And his answer is bittersweet, because though I know our baby deserves the world, his answer doesn't include me at all, and I look down at the little girl in Axel's arms. She has blue eyes, and I wonder if they'll turn lighter or darker. Summer skies or stormy seas.

"What should we name her?" Axel asks, and for a moment none of it matters, it doesn't matter if Axel and I get together or how my heart might break, because this *baby* is what matters.

"Jasmine," I say, the first name to come to mind.

"Little Jazz," Axel grins, and I notice that she already

has her daddy wrapped around her little finger–quite literally, because she won't let go of his thumb.

My throat works before I speak again.

"What about...what about *us*, Axel?" I ask, but then that's when the crew comes in, all of Jack and the Spades, including Gemma.

Gemma coos over the baby, scolding me for not keeping in touch with her. And I realize how much my past, my misgivings, my fears made me miss out on.

Gemma rubs her giant belly and smiles at me. "You beat me to the punch, but not for long, so the kiddos will grow up together. Like cousins. So, who's next in the Spades to have a baby?" Gemma asks. "My money's on Sammy."

Samuel blushes a bright pink. "Hush, I just now got a girlfriend."

Everything's changed so much since Axel and I split that I don't know which end is up.

Jackson, Locke, and Axel whoop and holler, and I shield Jasmine's ears, thinking that she'll be frightened. Instead, she just looks around, as if she's used to noise already. I guess it's all the time I spent listening to loud music when she was in my belly.

"She's a little rockstar already," Locke says. "I can't wait to have this little guy out so we can try for a princess next. What do you say, little bit?"

"You don't get to choose ahead of time, Locke," Gemma says dryly. Jackson's sitting in the corner, looking pale. I'm not sure what's going on with him, but it seems like something.

"Good to see you, Jack," I call to him, smiling slightly, and he gives me a genuine smile back, coming over to my bedside.

"Harley, you look gorgeous," he whispers in my ear, and Axel frowns.

"I heard that," Axel tells him.

"Good, you should. Your wife is a beautiful, brave woman, and someone should tell her," Jackson teases, winking at me.

"Ex-wife," Axel murmurs, and wow, *that's* a little arrow through my heart. In all the excitement, I'd almost forgotten that Axel and I haven't technically made up. I don't know how he's feeling or what he's thinking, and there are too many people here for me to ask now.

My heart drops to my toes when Axel goes out into the hall with the Spades, leaving me with Jasmine lying in the low bassinet near the bed.

"How are we going to keep your daddy?" I ask her quietly, and Jasmine grunts in her sleep. "No help, I see."

No matter what happens, I'm going to get Axel back. I'll explain to him everything, how my parents fucked me up when I was young, how my father's issues with infidelity gave me trust issues, how I was jealous and stupid and didn't give him enough credit. I'll beg for him to come home on my hands and knees, if I have to, even though I couldn't exactly do that right after surgery.

Axel still doesn't talk about it, even when Jasmine gets to go home later that day and he's strapping her into the car seat. She has her eyes wide open, unlike most newborns, looking around like she's excited to meet the day.

"I don't know if you should take her home, Axel," I say, nervous about being alone in the hospital.

"I know that you'll miss her, Harley, but you need to get some rest." He pauses. "And I need some time with her alone, just to get to know her, you know?"

It occurs to me that the only reason he would need to

get to know her on his own is if he planned on us splitting up and co-parenting, and I swallow, hard.

Maybe it's over. Axel doesn't seem angry, and that's worse than if he yelled at me every day. Dream Axel wasn't angry, either, but he didn't want me. Maybe *real* Axel doesn't want me anymore, either, after what I've done.

Honestly, I can't blame him. I guess I better get started trying to get down on my knees to beg.

Chapter 27

Axel

The next few days go by in a blur, because I don't sleep and I don't have any help with Jasmine. Gemma offers, but I tell her no, telling myself that I have to get used to doing it. Harley won't be well when she gets home, and I need to figure out all the new parent stuff for the both of us.

Jasmine misses her mama, though, and as soon as dusk falls, she begins to scream and cry. Harley isn't able to breastfeed due to the sudden surgery and blood loss, so Jazz is on the bottle.

She won't take it at all the first night, and I have to call Gemma for help. I can't very well call my sister, since she has no idea that I even have a baby.

"Wet a cloth with some warm water with just a little sugar in it," Gemma suggests. "That'll make her hungry and then she'll take the bottle."

It sounds crazy to me, giving my daughter sugar water like she's a damn hummingbird, but it works like a charm, and we both fall asleep on the couch while I'm watching a concert on television. Jasmine loves loud music, just like her parents, it turns out, because she can't fall asleep without some kind of music on in the background.

She has all these little quirks and eccentricities, just like any grown human being, and I get to know her in the three days that Harley's in the hospital.

On the second day, when I take her to visit her mother, Harley pouts at me.

"You're getting to know her better than I do," she complains.

"You've had nine months to get to know her," I say, and end up storming out of the room when she looks away.

Okay, so I'm still mad. I see no reason that Harley has kept this from me. I have always been upfront about how much I want her back, even after I found out that she was pregnant. It feels like a betrayal, and I hate it. But I can't very well fight with Harley while she's in a hospital gown, still looking pale and too thin after the baby was born.

Besides, it's not like I'm going anywhere. Harley knows that.

The second and final night that Jasmine and I spend alone together goes better than I expected, even though she still starts screaming, like clockwork, at dusk. I suppose that's when she realizes that something's missing, that Harley isn't with us, and I feel the loss too.

"I miss her too, Jazz bug," I tell her. "I've missed her a lot longer than you have. She'll be home tomorrow."

I've been staying in Harley's duplex, and I've moved in basically all my things while Gemma kept an eye on Jasmine. She's more than willing to help saying she needs the practice, and I couldn't be more thankful.

Gemma's given me some paternity leave, which is good

given that we have a big concert coming up in Vegas. Jasmine will be three weeks old, and Harley will be home, but I still can't imagine leaving them. I might still be angry at Harley, but I still don't want to be apart from her. I never have.

I sing songs that I wrote for Harley to our daughter, and she kicks around in her crib as if she's dancing. I can't wait to show Harley all the little things she does when she's at home. I can't wait until she's home, *period*. I miss her more than I thought possible, especially now that Jasmine is here.

It feels like there's a hole in our little family, something missing, and both Jasmine and I are excited to pick Harley up the next day.

I help Harley into the car, being careful with her, but she still winces when she gets into the backseat. It's just around dusk, and this time, instead of screaming, Jasmine's sleeping like the baby she is with Harley's hand resting on the top of her head.

I don't talk much on the way home, but that's because I'm *exhausted* and trying to keep my vision from doubling the road. Harley's quiet, too, so I assume she's tired.

When we arrive at the duplex, Harley bites at her lip, waiting for me to take Jasmine inside and come back and help her. I take her hand and she looks up at me from beneath her long eyelashes, her blue eyes wide.

"Are you going to take an Uber?" she asks, and I frown.

"To where? I got formula for Jasmine."

Harley doesn't answer, smiling a little, and when I scoop her up gently, bridal style, her arms go around my neck easily.

"So, you're staying here?" Harley asks, looking around at all my things.

"Obviously?" I tilt my head in her direction. "How else would I help with Jasmine?"

Harley huffs out a breath. "Where are you going to sleep?"

I stare at her. The duplex is one-story so it doesn't have stairs, and Harley can easily get into the bed. I have no idea what the hell she's talking about.

"In the bed?"

Harley nods, looking down, and I stare at her for another moment before taking Jasmine out of the car seat and putting her into the crib that's in the living room, the one that I set up.

Time goes by quickly, and Harley barely speaks, other than to laugh and smile at Jasmine, looking tired and still pale. Around dusk, just like I thought, Jasmine doesn't make a noise, not crying even a little.

Harley takes the blanket down from the top of the couch, lying down, and I look at her quizzically.

"Getting tired," she says, yawning. "I think I'll go to bed."

I nod, assuming that she wants to be in the same room with Jasmine, so when the baby falls asleep, I sit down in the recliner and doze off myself.

I hear Harley calling for me in a few hours, and she's managed to sit up on her own, which the doctor told her *not* to do.

"Harley, stop it! You'll pull your sutures," I warn her, and Harley favors me with a half-smile.

"You slept in here with us," she says, as if surprised.

"Of course I did. You can't pick up the baby on your own, silly," I tell her, and her face falls.

The next few days go by in an almost-haze, since I have to do all of the night feedings and still have to help Harley around the house. She asks me, hesitantly, on the fifth day that Jasmine's home, if I can help her shower.

"Yeah, just let me put bug to sleep," I tell her.

Jasmine goes down easily and Harley insists on walking herself to the bathroom, although I can tell it pains her to get up into the bath. I could have just carried her, but she seems adamant she should do it alone.

"I'll have to get used to it," she says softly, and I think that she means that she needs to keep her strength up, which I agree with.

"Turn around," she tells me when she is about to slide her nightie down, and I roll my eyes but I humor her. I suppose she doesn't want me to see the scars, but I will soon enough. Two months will be over in no time and I can't wait to see her after-baby body, but she seems insecure and so I keep my eyes averted as I help her wash her hair and get dressed again.

"Okay?" I ask her as she's leaning against the doorjamb, panting a little.

She smiles at me. "Thank you, for all this, Axel. I know that you would probably be somewhere else."

I snort. "There's nowhere else I'd rather be. My daughter is here."

Harley nods, and there's something a little sad in her face.

"Are you in pain?" I ask her, and she nods slightly, so I go to get her pain medication from the living room. When I return, she's made it all the way to the crib, looking down at Jasmine as she lies there, kicking her feet. She doesn't like to be swaddled, much to our chagrin.

"You shouldn't walk so far," I nag, and she nods, still looking down at our baby.

"We did something right," she says, and I put my arm

around her shoulders. She stiffens, seeming surprised, and then leans against me.

As far as I'm concerned, everything's right in my world. *Finally.*

Chapter 28

Harley

It's certainly bittersweet, having Axel there for two weeks while I'm healing. He often falls asleep in the recliner, watching over me and Jasmine, and it makes my heart soar, but I know that when I'm better enough to lift her, he'll be gone. He's given no indication that he wants to work things out, and I'm afraid to bring it up around Jasmine. I don't want to burst into tears, thinking that it will frighten her.

So I cry by myself, sometimes in the bathroom, sometimes on the couch, turned away from Jasmine and Axel, holding in my sobs so that they catch in my chest. It's hard, knowing that it's over but having him so close, and I wonder if this is how he felt when he first moved into the duplex next door.

The second week, I get my staples taken out at the doctor, having Charlotte drive me so that Axel can get some sleep with Jasmine. He wakes as I'm leaving.

"Oh, shit, your appointment!" he curses, sitting straight up.

I push a hand against his chest. "It's fine, I've got Charlotte taking me."

He relaxes, and then frowns. "You didn't want me to go? I wanted to hear what the doctor had to say."

I smile. That's sweet of him, to still care so much despite us not being together. "I'll tell you when I get back. Sleep while she's sleeping, okay?"

He huffs a little but lies back in the recliner, and he's snoring when Charlotte arrives to pick me up.

"How are things going?" Charlotte asks me when she helps me into the passenger seat, and I wince, but not from anything physical.

"Fine. Jasmine's an angel, and Axel is so good with her."

Charlotte stares at me. "I meant with you and Axel, you goob. What'd he say when you told him it was his? You haven't told me nearly *anything,*" she whines, pouting at me.

I shrug. "There's nothing to tell. He took me home and he's been staying long enough for me to get my staples out."

"He... he said that? That he was just going to leave when you could pick her up?" Charlotte looks at me incredulously.

"Well... *no*, not explicitly, but I can tell he's still mad at me."

"Just because he's still mad doesn't mean he's going to abandon you and your baby, Harls."

I think for a moment. That's a good point, but I can't imagine Axel staying for longer when we can't be together. When I'm healed again, my sex drive is going to come back, and I'm not sure that I can control myself.

"I don't think it's a good idea for him to stay," I admit.

"Why? I thought that you were coming around to the

idea of getting back together?" Charlotte asks, pulling out onto the interstate.

"I would love to get back together, but that's not what he wants. Not after what I did. How I lied."

Charlotte raises an eyebrow at me, but she doesn't say anything else. She's my best friend, and she knows when I don't want to talk about something.

Everything goes well at the doctor, although it doesn't feel good to get those stitches taken out, and I'm glad Charlotte talked me into taking a couple of pain pills before the appointment. They make me feel fuzzy and a little out of it, but I'll just be at home with Axel and Jasmine. Hopefully, he won't leave until they wear off.

"You're crazy, Harley," Charlotte says, and I realize that I've said that out loud. "He's not going to leave."

"I hope he never does," I mumble, feeling lightheaded and giving her a lopsided grin.

Charlotte laughs. "You're flying high on that pain medication, huh? Not used to taking double?"

"The doctor said that I could, but I never have," I admit, rolling my head around on my shoulders. It makes me dizzy, so I stop, looking out the window at the sky instead.

Charlotte helps me into the house because I'm a little unsteady on my feet, and Axel meets me at the door, looking refreshed and rested.

"Axel!" I cry out, all but falling into his arms, and he laughs.

"She had to take double her meds before the staples came out, so she's feeling no pain," Charlotte says with a wink.

"It didn't hurt that much," I say, although it certainly had. It just seems like a faint memory now, with the medication coursing through my blood.

"All right, lightweight. Let's get you to the couch."

"Bed," I say with a pout. "Take me to bed."

Axel raises an eyebrow, but he scoops me up into his arms and I sigh happily, wrapping my arms around his neck. I've always loved it when he carries me like this, like I weigh barely anything. For a girl who'd been considered chubby most of her life, it is a dream.

He lies me down gently on the bed, but I hang on to his wrist, tugging him down with me.

Axel makes an *oof* sound as he plops down on the bed.

"Will you hold me? Just while Jazz is sleeping?" At first, I'd hated the nickname Jazz, but now, it's growing on me.

Axel doesn't speak, just grunts, probably in irritation, and lies behind me, looping an arm around my waist. I wiggle to get closer to him and he backs away.

I make a whining sound in the back of my throat.

"Keep wiggling like that and I'll be poking you in the ass, Harls," he jokes, and a grin spreads across my face.

"You still want me?" I ask him, turning around to look at him with wide eyes.

Axel looks puzzled. "Fucking A, I do. What the hell?"

I laugh, feeling dizzy. "I wish you didn't hate me," I tell him, my bottom lip turning out in a pout.

Axel barks out a laugh. "I've never hated you, sweetheart. Not even when I tried."

"You should," I tell him, my eyes welling with tears. "I fucked up. I lied to you."

"You did," he agrees, wrapping his arm around my waist tighter. It doesn't hurt because he does it just below my breasts, above the surgery scar. He's gentle even when he brings me closer, and it makes me blubber and whimper. "Harley, what's wrong?"

"I love you," I gasp out between sobs and turn over and bury my face in his chest. "I love you and I'm so sorry."

Axel rubs my back in circles, chuckling softly. "You're just high, Harls, don't worry. Everything's fine."

"Everything's *not* fine," I insist. "You're leaving today, and I don't know what I'm going to do without you."

"I'm leaving? That's news to me," Axel says, and his blue eyes are sparkling with mirth when he looks at me.

"Don't make fun," I say glumly. "It's not nice to tease."

Axel moves his mouth close to my ear. "If I was teasing, you'd know, sweetheart."

A shiver runs down my spine. "What does that mean? You still want to hook up?"

"I don't think you're in any condition to hook up right now, Harls."

"I will be," I insist eagerly, hoping against hope. "We could go back to the way things were, when you moved into the duplex."

Axel frowns. "What, back when you were driving me crazy making me think you were fucking someone else?"

My face falls. " Yeah. I guess that wouldn't work."

Axel doesn't respond but he keeps rubbing my back. "We work just fine right now, sweetheart. Don't worry. And when you're better, I'll show you what I mean by teasing."

I frown, confused tears springing to my eyes again. "I don't understand. Won't you be leaving when I get better?"

Axel blinks, pulling away from me to focus on my face. "Do you want me to leave?"

"No! God, no," I admit, sniffling.

"Then why would I leave, sweetheart? I've got everything I want right here."

I don't know what he means, and my fuzzy brain is making things seem even more confusing. "Axel, I'm sorry.

I'm so sorry for everything, and I want you to stay. Not just until I'm better. Forever."

Axel looks at me, and I continue, almost babbling. "I want you to stay here with me and Jazz, for us to get married again. Don't you think it'd be good for her to have two parents who were together? You could learn to love me again, Axel, right?"

Axel's smiling at me, but I have no idea what he's going to say. Instead of speaking, he just leans forward to kiss me, softly, and that doesn't answer any of my questions at all.

Chapter 29

Axel

The Vegas concert comes up before I realize it, with everything being a blur between Harley getting better and Jasmine. I haven't slept much the last week, but I manage to snooze on the tour bus, the same one that Gemma rented for us for the last tour.

The Vegas show is just a gig, not part of a tour. I've got too much going on for that, although Jack and the Spades will still be performing locally, and Jackson's still planning to release that solo album.

Our next tour will be planned when none of us have small babies, much to Jackson's chagrin.

"Everyone's wrapped up in love and not music," he grumbles.

"Love *is* music," Gemma says brightly, and Jackson snorts.

I'm excited, having not picked up my guitar other than to play songs for Jasmine, trying to get her to sleep. It hadn't worked very well. She just seemed to kick and coo more when I played instead of falling asleep, but I guess that was her rockstar blood.

"How are the girls?" Locke asks me when we're about to start rehearsal, and I grin brightly.

"Jasmine's already about to start crawling, I can just tell. Harley says it's way too early, but I think my baby girl is a genius. She's already starting to try to roll over in her crib." Locke grins at me while I go on and on about Jasmine, talking about her blue eyes beginning to widen and brighten, how much she looks like her mother.

"I can't wait for that to be me too."

"I'm tired as all hell, but loving every second of it," I say, and Locke snorts.

"Not looking forward to that part."

Rehearsal goes well, only a few technical difficulties from the amps being the wrong size, but Samuel has an adapter. His hair has started to grow out, and things with his girl seem to be going well. They're even talking about moving in together, this early.

"Whipped," Locke and I say at the same time, and Samuel doesn't blush this time, just grins and nods.

Jackson's been MIA so much we never see him unless it's time for a rehearsal or a concert, and he's quiet, almost snappy as he's getting us all ready.

"Who put a stick up your ass?" Locke asks, and Samuel and I laugh.

Jackson narrows his eyes at us. "You three."

We all goof around until it's time for the concert, and I'm not taking tequila shots or even drinking beer on stage, this time. Talking with Locke has made me miss Jasmine viscerally, but luckily, I get to see her eyes in the crowd.

Harley's standing with Gemma, front and center, in a smoking hot red club dress that I can't wait to rip off her later, in the hotel room. She's holding a mojito in one hand and her phone in the other, filming for social media.

Harley said that in order for us not to fight, Sophie had to go, so she's probably in the concert hall somewhere, but I can't talk with her one on one anymore. I told Harley that was fair enough, as long as she never so much as looked at that Roland square again, and she agreed.

I used my money from the tour and my salary to buy the duplex that we'd been in, and we plan on knocking down the wall between them when Jasmine is a bit older. Harley's father had put in an offer, too, but luckily Harley had an in with Theresa at the real estate office, and she slid our offer into the higher-ups.

When I perform "Amped Up," the hard partying song that I'd written just after Harley and I split, I look right at her, grinning. She jumps up and down, still my hard rock girl.

I'd been worried about finding a sitter, but Harley had *insisted*, saying she needed to feel like my wife again and not just a mother, and since we'd had to get married at the courthouse instead of having another big wedding due to buying the house, I agreed.

Charlotte is a good sitter, anyway, and she knows both our numbers in case something happens.

As the concert ends, Jackson and Locke are called away immediately. Turns out, Gemma wanted to work until her last pregnant day and the concert was the last straw. Her waters broke as the last note sounded and they drove her to the hospital, arguing the whole time over who would do what until they left. We promise to go to visit in the morning.

Harley's tipsy. When we get back to the hotel, her hands are all over me. It's not time for us to be sexually active again, but Harley slides down my body, getting on her knees in the elevator with a wicked grin.

193

Callie Stevens

"You deserve a reward for how good you did on stage, baby," she purrs, raking her nails down my thighs through my jeans, and when she takes me into her mouth I rock my head back, pressing the emergency button on the elevator.

We might be married again after a nine-month break, but right now, I'm just a rockstar, and she's just a groupie.

A groupie that I hope follows me around for the rest of our lives.

Chapter 30

Axel

Epilogue

I still can't believe how lucky I am to have both Harley and Jazz as my family.

Life with the two of them has been heaven and hell all at once.

Heaven because I'm exactly where I want to be, with my woman in my arms every night and my baby girl filling up my heart to the brim. It is amazing to see that there is no limit to the love I have for these two, and that surprisingly, it grows and grows, every single day.

But it is also hell, not only because Jazz is testing our abilities to function with little to no sleep –little girl is a night owl and loves noise and music at all times of the day and night—but also Harley's body tempts me every time she is the room with me. Even just her smell when I walk into a room she has been is enough to get me hard these days. And it kills me that there is nothing I can do to claim her, because the doctor hasn't cleared her yet, and won't clear her for weeks still.

And then it hits me. This is Vegas!

"I'm taking a shower and then I'm sleeping like the

dead. Charlotte is an angel for taking Jazz for the night and I'm taking full advantage of it."

"Enjoy, sweetheart. Take a bath if you feel like it. I know how you love soaking up."

"Choices, choices..." She laughs as she heads to the bathroom, and as soon as she closes the door I reach into my pocket and send a couple of text messages.

After I make sure my girl is tucked in and passed out, I take a quick shower and silently leave the room. I have a few things to take care of.

Chapter 31

Harley

Epilogue

I wake up to someone knocking on my door.

"Axel, can you get that?" I say before I even open my eyes. I'm not ready to wake up yet. There is no answer and my hand reaches out to wake him up, but all I find is cold sheets and an empty bed beside me. What the hell?

"Coming," I yell, checking my phone to see the time. I groan. It's barely nine AM. It was already past four in the morning when I fell asleep. I wanted to sleep to my heart's content today, since Charlotte has Jazz, but apparently, the universe hates me.

Getting out of bed, I head to the door and open it to find a smiling and very perky Charlotte with a bag on her hands. "Are you kidding me, right now? Where is Jazzie?"

"Oh, don't worry about her, she's with her daddy, so she is happy as can be. We need to hurry because we have places to go an people to see."

"Nope! The only place I want to see today is the inside of my bed, so shoo." I try to throw her out of the room, but she is not budging. So stubborn!

"Come on," she pulls me to where my clothes are. "Get dressed and hurry up. We have an appointment in twenty minutes."

I have no idea what she is talking about, but maybe if I humor her, I can come back to bed and sleep in a bit. "Fine." I throw some skinny jeans and a T-shirt on and put my hair up in a messy bun. Less than five minutes later, I'm ready to leave.

She leads me down the elevator to the hotel salon. A couple of chairs are already waiting for us with what looks like a team of people. Not a single mirror in sight. I squint at Charlotte and she just grins at me. "Beauty treatment day, compliments of your guy." I can't help but smile at that. He knows how much I miss having some me time, so he arranged this. When I thought I couldn't love him more, he goes and does this.

We sit, and for an hour, people fuss over our hair and do our make-up and we get mani-pedis and face masks and the whole shebang. All the while, we are treated with mimosas and I feel like royalty. I missed this.

Finally, they claim we are done, and Charlotte comes to me and says, "Now you have to trust me. Can you do that?"

Frowning, I tentatively say, "I guess..."

She pulls out a blindfold and tries to put it on me. "What the hell are you doing? Are you crazy?"

"Trust me," she urges. Guess Axel's plan is not done yet, so signing, I indulge her.

Blind as a bat due to the fabric over my eyes, I'm led somewhere and she asks me to undress.

"No! I don't even know where I am! I trust you, but there is no way I'm getting naked only God knows where and in front of God knows who. Nuh-uh."

"Don't be ridiculous. Spread your arms." I do, and I can

touch what feel like really cold smooth walls all around me. Like glass or mirrors. "This is a dressing room," she says. "Now do as I say or we'll be late."

I take off my clothes and she helps me get into a tight, fitted dress. Is he taking me out on a surprise date? It's been so long since we've gone on a date. Any date.

Clothes, and shoes all handled, she takes me by the hand, still blindfolded and blind as can be. When we stop, I can hear the click of a door opening and we get inside wherever she is taking me.

It is not a restaurant, too quiet. Where the hell am I?

"Ready, Harls?"

"For what? I have no idea what is going on."

"Here goes nothing," Charlotte says. And her hands touch my blindfold taking it off.

For a few seconds, light blinds me and my eyes blink like crazy. When I can finally see again, my breath wooshes out of me.

Axel is wearing a suit and tie and holding Jazz who is wearing a beautiful white dress. Looking down at me for the first time. Pearly white shoes, pearly white dress. Ohmygod! Ohmygod! Ohmygod!

Tears come to my eyes as Charlotte takes place right beside—is that Theresa? She waves at me. Sammy is right next to Axel, also in a suit and he is holding a phone where Jackson, Locke, and Gemma's faces are smiling at me. Gemma is holding her newborn baby and looks equal parts happy and exhausted.

Axel comes to me, kneels and says, "Harley, sweetheart, I love you more than words can tell. My feelings for you are something that can't even be put into words and having you in my life turns my days into a never-ending melody that I want to be part of the soundtrack of my life forever. I know this might seem out of the blue and sudden and crazy, but you would make me the happiest man on Earth if you would please give me the honor, the privilege of becoming my wife. Right now."

Tears are now tracking down my face and I can only hope I'm wearing waterproof makeup. I can't speak, so I just nod and nod and nod, a giant grin on my face,

He rises, offering his arm to me. "Shall we?"

I take his arm and together we walk down the aisle.

Vows are exchanged, and tears are spilled, and when I finally hear, "I now pronounce you husband and wife," I know this second chance is my long-awaited happily ever after with the man I have always loved and will forever love.

"You may now kiss the bride."

Looking into Axel's eyes, I wait until his lips take mine and I'm finally home.

Thank you for reading Accidental Secret Daddy.

If you loved this book, then you'll love Secret Baby For My Best Friend's Brother...

Read on for a preview...

Secret Baby For My Best Friend's Brother

Preview

My best friend's brother took my V card four years ago and left a bun in the oven.

One night of passion was all it took to change my life forever.

He doesn't remember, but I can't forget it.

When I'm given the job opportunity of a lifetime I can't turn it down.

Even if it means coming face-to-face with him.

All I have to do is not fall for him...*again*.

And keep the biggest secret of my life under wraps.

When I see Jackson again, I am melted in his sea-green eyes.

It takes everything in me to not pull him in for a kiss...or more.

Watching him play with my son sparks emotions I thought I dealt with long ago.

They are like two peas in a pod, my son even has his green eyes.

I'm so close to having everything I ever wanted, but at what cost?

One night of passion, four years of lies, I have one chance to fix this.

Or I lose my Rockstar forever...

Continue to read Secret Baby For My Best Friend's Brother...

Chapter 1

Jackson

"I'm hiring a stylist," Gemma says, and I look up from the notebook I'm scribbling lyrics in.

"A stylist? Why?" I ask. We've always worn whatever we wanted, and we certainly hadn't had a stylist on tour.

"Because you all look like a bunch of Nirvana rejects, that's why," Gemma explains dryly.

I shake my head, smiling a little. "Don't pull punches on account of me," I joke.

"We need a more cohesive style for this next concert. I know you've been focused on the new album, and I'm proud of you, but Jack and the Spades needs to ride this popularity high for as long as we can," my sister continues.

"It's not my fault we ended up taking two breaks from touring and only did the gigs. Blame that on Locke and Axel, they're the fertile ones," I scoff. "You don't catch *me* getting anyone pregnant with a rug rat."

Cain rolls over on his blanket on the floor and squeals at me, as if reminding me that I love the little rug rat.

I coo at him and go over to pick him up, sitting him on my knee as I write. He grabs at my pen and kicks around.

Chapter 1

"Fine. Do you have anyone in mind?" I ask, and Gemma grins.

"Yeah, actually. My best friend from high school, remember her?"

I vaguely remember a mousy, petite girl who used to hang around Gemma all the time, but barely.

"Sure," I lie, and Gemma rolls her eyes.

"Susie Carmichael, remember?"

"Sure," I say again, although the name doesn't ring any bells.

"She goes by her middle name now, Zoe," Gemma says, and I freeze.

Zoe isn't exactly an uncommon name, I suppose, but it still stings to think about the girl I met while we were on tour.

Meeting a girl on tour that I connected with more than any other woman wasn't something that I expected, but here I am. I tried and tried to convince Gemma to stay in Albuquerque another couple of days, but the tour had to go on, and luckily, my blue-haired goddess Zoe followed suit.

So, I snuck around the entire tour, sneaking Zoe into my hotel rooms, stealing kisses at breakfast before the others got up, picking her up on the sink in dirty club bathrooms. She deserved better, and I wanted to give that to her.

She bit down on her bottom lip when I asked her to come to Tucson and for us to make a real go of it.

"We've got a good thing going now, Jackson. We have fun together, don't we?"

I'd swayed toward her, not drunk on tequila but on her, the way she smelled like cherry blossoms and whiskey. I tried to put my arms around her waist but she backed away, into the elevator.

"Yeah, we have fun, but what if it's more than that, Zoe?

Chapter 1

What if we could be good together? Give me your number, at least."

Zoe was standing in the elevator, about to go up to her room, and she gave me a sly smile.

"You wouldn't call me," she said, and pressed the button. I stared at her until the doors closed, and she kept that sly smile.

So, I don't have her number, or even her last name. We hooked up over half a dozen times on tour, but she didn't give me any identifying information. The only thing I know is that her name is Zoe, and she has a four-year-old son who I'd met only twice, while we were in Dallas.

His name is Elijah and he's smart as a whip, and adorable, too, just like her. He has her dark hair, and he likes music, too, and classic rock, of all things. I never considered dating a single mom, but Elijah is something else and it makes me wonder. I'm nearing thirty and all my friends are having kids, so maybe someone like Zoe would be good for me, would help me to settle down without having to have a kid of my own.

It hadn't been just a fling for me, and I tried to tell her that the last night, but she'd gone up in the elevator and out of my life as if it meant nothing at all.

I frown down at my notebook, thinking of how I needed a sultry female voice to sing the backup lines, and remembering Zoe's sweet, alto tone when she had sung along with my songs.

"Jack?"

I shake my head, ridding myself of thoughts of Zoe. My Zoe and this Zoe are two different people, after all, and I need to focus on the band and on our music. Maybe it's for the best that we didn't end up hooking up back at home.

I know I have the tendency to fall hard, and I don't need

to be distracted right now, since the Spades are going on their second national tour.

We're starting in Santa Fe, this time, with Axel's return from paternity leave, and being close to our hometown should mean that there's a *lot* of fans. Gemma's right: we need a stylist to give us something unique.

"Sorry. Just thinking about the album," I say, even though that's partially a lie.

"What's wrong?"

I shake my head. "Nothing. I just haven't found a backup singer just yet."

Gemma frowns slightly, and I can almost see the wheels turning in her head. She's frugal when it comes to spending the band's money, so I'd planned to hire someone for just a few hours a week to do the backup lines out of my own pocket.

"So, when are you gonna hire her?" I ask, changing the subject, and Gemma smirks.

"I already did."

"You weren't even gonna run it by me?" I ask, and Gemma pouts a little.

"I just did."

Damn, my sister is hardheaded. Strong-willed is an understatement, and sometimes, I feel sorry for my best friend for having married her. She's a great girl, but she doesn't listen.

I chuckle, shaking my head. "Fair enough. When does she start?"

"Tonight," Gemma says simply. "We have a gig tomorrow, so we need someone right away, right?"

"And the fact that she's your best friend doesn't have anything to do with this, right?"

Chapter 1

Gemma frowns. "No, not really. I haven't talked to her in years, after all. We lost touch after high school. I saw her again in the supermarket and asked her what she was up to. Remember, she was already interested in design when we were kids."

I nod as if I remember, but to be honest, I don't. I was kind of a mess back then. After all those years of abuse our parents had put us through, their death was at the same time a bit of a relief and added pressure. Barely out of high school, I now had to grieve my abusive parents and support myself and my little sister. Not that that was much different than before. I was always trying to find odd jobs since I was about twelve to make sure both me and Gemma had something to eat most days, since all my parents cared about was where to find their next hit, be it booze or drugs. I had to become an adult really fucking fast and my sister, as always, depended on me. Except now, I was all she had. Those were difficult times and there was a lot going on, so everything was sort of a haze.

"She's coming to meet everyone tonight at dinner, so you better be there." Gemma points at me, pulling me out from my trip down shitty memory lane.

Bossy.

I know better than to say that, though. "Sure, I'll be there. The diner?"

"Where else?" Gemma grins. The diner was her favorite place to get all her pregnancy cravings met, and she still seems to have the same tastes. French toast and French onion soup seem like an odd combination to me, but what do I know?

"All right, now get out," Gemma demands, and I blink at her.

"You're kicking me out?"

Chapter 1

"Yep. Zoe's coming over so we can ride together, and I don't want you distracting her."

I stare at her blankly. "Why would I distract her?"

Gemma rolls her eyes. "You really don't remember her, do you? She never said anything, but the way she sometimes looked at you, I could swear she had the *biggest* crush on you when we were growing up."

I grin. "Oh?"

"Don't you dare." Gemma points at me again. "You keep it in your pants, Jackson Arden, or I swear to God—"

"Okay, okay!" I laugh. I don't have any designs on Gemma's friends, anyway. I'm still reeling from meeting *my* Zoe and hoping that I'll see her blue hair somewhere in the crowd at the concert tomorrow.

I stand up, sliding my notebook into my back pocket, and that's when a car pulls up in the driveway.

I don't pay any attention, looking around for my keys, until I hear a small squeak.

When I look up, there's a blue-haired goddess standing in our garage.

My face goes pale. She looks pale, also, rubbing a hand across the back of her neck.

"Hello, Jackson."

My Zoe is Gemma's Zoe.

What the *fuck?*

Continue to read Secret Baby For My Best Friend's Brother...

Chapter 2

Zoe

I'm stupid.

This is a well-known fact to me, but I'm *particularly* stupid about Jackson Arden, and I lose all rational thought when he's in my general vicinity. It's been that way since I was fifteen and I had a huge crush on my best friend's brother, and it extended to now, at twenty-two, as well.

The thing about Jackson Arden is that he's one of the most responsible people I've ever met, while also being the biggest mess I've ever met. He takes care of his little sister, Gemma, my best friend, like she's his own daughter, even though he's only a few years older than her. He must have been just as devastated as Gemma after his parents' death, but he'd stepped up to take care of her, done everything that he could to raise her right, while also hard partying while working two or three jobs to support them.

There's this maturity in him that has always been fascinating to me. He's the only guy I've ever met who was like that, and it attracted me immediately. I guess some things never change.

I already knew that I am still stupid about Jackson,

given that he'd winked at me *once* at the first concert I'd seen him at back in Dallas and I'd ended up in his hotel room the next morning. Then I'd done it *again*, taking him to my place, which was extra stupid given that my babysitter brought Elijah back too early the next morning.

I'd been terrified of them meeting, of course, terrified that Jackson would notice something, but he hadn't. He'd been good with Elijah, singing along to The Who when Elijah showed him his little Walkman that I'd bought him..

Elijah and Jackson had their music taste in common, and many other things as well. Elijah had his eyes and his smile, too, because Elijah is *his*.

When Jackson hit on me in Dallas, at first, I was offended that he didn't recognize me, but I'd grown up from the seventeen-year-old girl with a crush.

I still remember the first thing he said to me that night.

"Susie, you're prettier than you think, you know?" He *had let go and was pretty drunk, swaying on his feet.*

Blushing, I put both hands on his chest to steady him. "Yeah? You've never noticed before."

His green eyes were bloodshot and hazy, but still beautiful when he looked down at me, grabbing my wrists with his hands when I tried to pull away.

"I'm noticing now."

He leaned down, and when his lips touched mine, I was lost.

I'd been lost since the moment we met when I was fifteen, if I was honest with myself, and now he was standing in front of me, frowning. Something like anger flashed in his green eyes and I licked my lips, my throat suddenly dry.

"Hello, Jackson."

He doesn't respond and Gemma nudges him with her shoulder.

Jackson sighs, not quite looking at me. "Hello, *Susie."*

Shit. He *is* mad. So what, I didn't tell him who I was when we first hooked up at the concert. Why would I? He didn't remember me, and I should have been pissed off enough not to hook up with him, but like I already established, I'm stupid about Jackson Arden, and I guess I always will be.

Besides, *I'm* the one who should be mad. At him. At what had happened years ago. And now, what, he's ashamed of me? Because I'm Gemma's friend?

I set my jaw, speaking through gritted teeth. "Good to see you again, Jackson," I say, and he nods before excusing himself to leave the garage, jumping in the same car he's had since high school.

It isn't like I didn't know I would have to see him again, but I was hoping he didn't react like *this.*

"What's his problem?" Gemma asks, and I shrug.

"How should I know? I just got here and he's *your* brother," I say shrugging, feigning ignorance. Because I do know. But I don't want to talk about it now.

Jackson has always been friendly and outgoing, which is one of the reasons I'd fallen for him. He's a natural flirt.

Gemma frowns but takes my hand, dragging me inside. "This is Cain," she says proudly, pointing at the baby rolling around on a blanket.

I grin, crouching down to look at him. "This is such a good age. Hi, big boy!"

Cain squeals up at me and I feel a pang in my heart, thinking of Elijah at this age.

"You've got one, too, right?" Gemma says. "Maybe we could have a playdate."

My smile fades. "Maybe. Elijah is a little older."

I'm being vague on purpose. Gemma is a lot more observant than Jackson.

Gemma waves a hand dismissively. "It'll be fine. Cain's a rough and tumble guy, aren't you, sweetie?"

Cain shouts something incoherent and Gemma laughs.

"He's a lot louder than his father. Gets it from me."

"Locke Kincaid, huh?" I ask, smiling at Gemma, and she has the grace to blush a little.

She shrugs. "What can I say? I guess I have a thing for older guys."

I snort. "Well, good for you."

Gemma and I hadn't stayed in touch after graduation. I had left town and never returned until now. I regret it. It's great seeing how happy she is, how she's squeezing my hand. It's good to have my best friend back, even if her brother is trouble for me.

"I figured we should start with Jackson, first," Gemma says, and I stiffen.

"Jackson? Why? He's pretty stylish."

"If you call ripped jeans and holey T-shirts stylish," Gemma groans. "Jack and the Spades have the whole grunge thing going on, and that's fine, but I want to find a way to make them come together more, you know?"

I nod, understanding exactly what she means. "Yeah, even if it's a casual style, you want them to kind of match."

Gemma gives me a bright smile. "Exactly." She pauses and then pulls me into a hug. She's a little taller than me so she rests her head on my shoulder. "I'm glad to have you back, Suze."

"Zoe," I remind her, and she shakes her head.

"That's going to take just a little getting used to. Be patient with me."

Chapter 2

I smile. "I will, no worries. So, we need to go shopping?" I ask, and Gemma's face falls.

"We do, but I can't go with you," she says mournfully. "I don't have anyone to watch the kiddo and he's a holy terror in public. I'm still breastfeeding," she explains.

My eyes widen. "Good for you. Elijah got teeth at four months, and I gave it up," I admit.

Gemma winces. "I'm glad I don't have to deal with that, just yet. Axel's wife says their little girl is already teething and she's a couple months older than Cain."

"Everyone's having babies," I muse, and Gemma nods. "Everyone but Jackson."

My mouth goes dry again. I want to tell Gemma about me and Jackson, but I can't. It's been years since we were best friends, so I just swallow the lump in my throat and remember once again ,that I'm playing with fire taking this job because he most definitely *does* have a baby, it's just that no one knows about it. And I don't want anyone to find out.

But: A. I need a job. Badly. I've been working as a waitress for four years now, and it's just not paying the bills. I've had to move back to New Mexico to stay with my parents because of my lack of funds. Designing is what I've always wanted to do, and this would be a step in the right direction. And B. I'm still stupid about Jackson Arden.

After we had our little fling on tour and he was so sweet and earnest, asking me if I wanted to come to Tucson, I can't stop thinking about him. Not that I ever have. Jackson Arden had been on my mind in one way or another since I was fifteen, and it looks like that's never going to change.

I don't lie to myself about my reasons. Part of me wants to be in Jackson's life, wants us to hook up again, and I can't deny that. Maybe that's why I gave in to him in Albuquerque that first night–or maybe it was the fact that I've

213

always wanted Jackson and he had only given me the time of day once, when I was seventeen, and I was starved for more. It had been stupid to even *go* to the concert, but when I saw an advertisement online about Jack and the Spades, I'd had to go.

The band had been in the early stages when I had last spoken to Gemma, and I'm proud of Jackson for bringing them so far. They were popular around the Midwest, now, and making good money. I always knew that Jackson would go places, but I hadn't imagined it would happen this quickly.

Gemma says they are working on a new album now, and my heart swells with pride for him, even if we barely know each other now. I don't deny that I still love him just as much as I did as a teenager. I just don't want him to know it.

"You're married now?" Gemma asks, and I scoff.

"The father ran off the second I told him I was pregnant," I explain, telling her the words I have been telling everyone.

Gemma sighs. " I'm so sorry, Su-Zoe."

"You're getting better at that already." I grin, and Gemma laughs, loud and open. I think I've missed her just as much as I've missed Jackson. Having a best friend would have helped wonders while I was pregnant with Elijah, but I'm glad I have her now.

Luckily, as a stylist, I'll be working with Gemma more than the guys. She makes it clear that she runs the show as their manager, and all I have to do is get their measurements and find some real rocker outfits for them.

"What are you thinking for the Tucson show?" Gemma asks, and I tilt my head, thinking.

"Leather. Leather pants, white T-shirts, leather jackets. Some of them can be graphic tees, if the guys want."

"I don't care what they want," Gemma jokes, although I'm not one hundred percent sure she's joking. "Whatever you decide for tomorrow night is what they'll wear."

I nod, trying to think of how I'm going to work my tiny budget into clothes for four guys.

Gemma rummages around in her purse on the floor and then stands up, handing me a credit card.

"Here's the business card. Try to keep it under five thousand for the first show, if you can," she says easily, and I gape at her, surprised.

"You guys really *are* doing well," I comment, and Gemma shrugs.

"We are, but I'm just frugal with money. I'm working on buying us a used tour van so we don't have the expense and deposit of renting it, and that'll save us a lot."

Gemma always was mature beyond her years, different than me. I'd always kind of flown by the seat of my pants, just going where the wind blew me and pursuing whatever passion I had at the time. For a few years, it had been designing clothes. Before that, it had been Jackson. Now, I need to reconcile the two of them. At least I won't be working with him closely.

"Do you still sing?" Gemma asks, and I frown a little, confused.

"I mean, not professionally. I kill it at karaoke, though."

Gemma giggles. "Well, do you think you could do a few lines as a backup on the album?"

I try not to visibly react. "Aw, Gemma, I'm a stylist, not a singer," I complain, and she sighs.

"I know, Jackson's just been really struggling with the last couple of songs, not having anyone. I was hoping I didn't have to hire someone else."

I think about some girl working closely with Jackson in

the studio, putting her hand on his bicep as they work, and I wrinkle my nose involuntarily.

"I'll give it a try, if you don't fire me after this first style," I joke.

What the hell am I doing? This is a bad idea. I shouldn't work so closely with Jackson, not after the way we were on the tour. It's only a few lines, though, right? I certainly don't want any other girl doing it, so I have no choice.

Jackson may not be mine, but I'll be damned if I let another girl slide in on him while I'm around.

Continue to read Secret Baby For My Best Friend's Brother...

Printed in Great Britain
by Amazon

18592888R00129